MW01077532

The Alien Tide

Tom Dongo

**Cover Art and Illustrations by
Joanna Heikens**

Published by
Hummingbird Publishing Co.
P.O. Box 2571
Sedona, AZ 86336

Copyright 1990 by Tom Dongo
ISBN 0-9622748-1-X

All rights reserved. No part of this book may be reproduced by any means or in any form, except brief quotes for literary reviews, without written permission from the author.

Printed by
Mission Possible Commercial Printing
a division of Light Technology Communication Services
P.O. Box 1495
Sedona, AZ 86336

Acknowledgment

Without the trusting and loving help of old and new friends this book could not have been written. To them all I extend my heartiest thanks.

And special thanks to Dr. Tom O'Donnell of Bradenton, Florida—now of Sedona.

Contents

Beneath the tides of sleep and time,
strange fish are moving.

Thomas Wolfe

*Life is either a great adventure
—or it is nothing at all.*

Helen Keller

CHAPTER 1

UFOs: Some Theories and Questions

As I began writing this book, I had feelings of reluctance and apprehension about even beginning a book on UFOs, because events and new information are coming so rapidly that I feared the book might be obsolete even before it got into print. This may yet prove to be the case. Time will tell.

Because of lengthy observations I have made concerning UFOs, I am thoroughly convinced that one of the two following events will take place within the next few years. Either of these events will completely change how we think and live on this planet.

The first is that interdimensional, spiritual, or extraterrestrial (or all three) beings will openly announce their presence on this planet. The second is that the U.S. government will voluntarily or involuntarily release the almost overwhelming information it has on UFOs and extraterrestrials, and the dealings it has had with them since the late 1940s.

After writing *Mysteries of Sedona*, which was reprinted five times the first year, I wanted to do another book. But on what subject? After a lot of deliberation, I settled on a book about UFOs, in part because my interest in the subject has become almost obsessive, and in part because UFO books have attained increased marketability. I decided to focus the theme of the book on UFO/ET/paranormal activity in the general area where I live—Sedona, Arizona. Sedona, I feel, is merely one slice of a big pie. Whatever is going on here is going on everywhere else, albeit by varying degrees.

When I began my research on the book in earnest (adding to the information I already had), I was not prepared for the magnitude and importance of the information I would subsequently uncover. As I dug deeper and deeper, I was not (and still am not) able to fully assimilate and comprehend the variety and enormity of alien-being and spaceship activity in this area and worldwide.

After interviewing numerous individuals—men, women, boys and girls from every level of society—and because of what I was discovering, I decided to expand the scope of the book to encompass the larger issues I had uncovered. In my probings I gradually gained the trust of many people. I would not have uncovered nearly enough to fill a book had not a network early established itself. Over one hundred incidents and individuals were referred to me through personal contacts I had made through this network.

In the beginning stages of this book I placed an ad in *Creative Happenings*, a local publication with a wide circulation in metaphysical circles. I was seeking anyone who had had ET or UFO experiences of any type, and I guaranteed complete anonymity to respondents. To my surprise, after a month I had not received even one reply. I learned that advertising was not the way to generate information and connections. Developing the trust and confidence of interviewees, I have found, plays a key role in an undertaking such as mine.

Some of those same interviewees are now some of my best friends. In most cases the names used in this book are not real names. I was either asked to keep identities confidential or I chose to for my own reasons.

In this book I am going to make no attempt to prove these entities exist. Rather, I am going on the premise that they *do* exist, and so what do we do now? I also have endeavored to present material in such a way that it does not turn people off or sound like I am trying to sensationalize the subject. Most UFO books out now attempt to build a case to validate the presence of these ETs or EBEs (extraterrestrial biological entities) here on our planet. I am saying (and most of you suspect it, anyway) that they are here—now, amongst us—and am proceeding from that conviction.

I have more than proven the existence of these beings to myself, and because I feel it is so important, I hope through the medium of this book to convince any skeptical reader so that they also have no doubt. Perhaps in these pages we can come to some conclusion as to why they are here. At the moment that is the paramount mystery—why *are* they here? And why are they here in such numbers?

I doubt that the reason they are here is to simply study a newly discovered, primitive, embryonic species—us. There is convincing evidence pointing to alien existence on Earth hundreds of millions of years ago, so we are not something new to them. I have come to the conclusion, after years of intense study, that the aliens know something critical that we don't! A disturbing amount of hard evidence in the form of released documents and high-ranking testimonies indicate that our government knows exactly what that something is, and they are not telling us for reasons known only to them. If the secret were divulged, would it result in mass panic or anarchy? Is our government allowing a small group of elite insiders to decide the affairs and fate of billions of people, all because of the extraterrestrial alien question?

I strongly believe there is some unknown (to us) element (radiation?) in our atmosphere that is accumulating and building toward a reactive state. I believe it is in some way not only harming *us* but some ETs as well. Have we raped and plundered this planet so badly that it is fast approaching a point of total collapse?

Then there is the hole in the ozone layer at the south pole, and now perhaps the north pole—the result of chlorofluorocarbons from freon coolants and aerosol sprays. The ozone crisis was on TV for a few weeks and now most people have all but forgotten it in the pressure of daily affairs. More than one prominent scientist has claimed that the spreading ozone hole may prove to be the death knell of this planet. The U.S. and several small countries have taken action and banned manufactured fluorocarbons—while the rest of the world still manufactures tons of the stuff daily, with full knowledge of what it is doing to the Earth's outer atmosphere. The world ignores UFO activity with the same attitude.

Are we—the human race, the infant race—losing control? Are superbeings here to keep us from doing any more damage? Nuclear war? Not likely. If the first button is pushed, they will be there! There are several reliable accounts in military circles of UFOs deactivating more than one nuclear warhead and rendering missile-activating systems useless. Some of these missiles and their systems were deactivated by UFOs while the missile sat in its silo under tons of concrete.

If you look at the whole UFO-ET scenario that has taken place, especially during the last thirty years, it seems depressingly negative. A host of recent books helps to leave one with that impression. Some of those books leave the reader with the feeling that the situation is hopeless. However, there is a bright side to the picture. There is great hope and opportunity equally present! Those who seize the enormous opportunity that is here now, an opportunity that perhaps has never been before, will abundantly prosper in the coming days.

Who are "they"? In my questioning, most of the contactees and abductees each had a measure of recollection of what type of being they had encountered. Interestingly enough, out of the different humanoid types described by witnesses, only a few types looked identical to humans. From global eyewitness accounts, we seem to have three (or more) close human relatives from the stars. One group is called the "Swedes." They are typically described as being beautiful, tall, with fair hair and complexion. The three "human" groups seem to be helping us as much as they can, but at the same time remaining in the background. They do not seem to want to be directly involved or to perhaps be responsible for problems that could arise from their appearance at this time. That could change very quickly, however. I firmly believe that when the crunch comes, these three or more human groups will come in to help us. That seems to be the definite pattern at present.

How do all these humanoids and humans remain unseen, seemingly invisible? The answer to that may be rather obvious. These beings are able to alter their vibrational pattern at will—all of them can. They are able to change their molecular structure so that they can vibrate at a different frequency from our own. They know how to manipulate energy efficiently. We don't—at least not yet. For example, we can hear (normally) at a rate of from 20 to 20,000 vibrations per second. We are unable to hear, for the most part, anything below or above that rate. We can see (normally) in the 4/10,000- (violet) to 7/10,000-millimeter (red) range. Beyond or below that rate our physical sight cannot perceive.

If one of those beings or ships is at a higher rate, it could be right in front of us and we would be unable to see or hear it. It may also be that most of them do not have a dense physical form. Because this is a reputed "third-density" system (as opposed to second, fourth, fifth, sixth, tenth, etc.), they may have to comply with the energy laws of our third-density system. It is at these times of compliance that they become visible to us.

CHAPTER 2

UFOs—My Involvement

In this chapter I will explain my background in all this. I think you will find some similarities to your own background of interest in UFOs and related phenomena. Perhaps you may find yourself depicted in these pages. It is my fervent hope that you, the reader, get "fired up" about UFOs and become personally involved. We all need to stay abreast of new information regarding UFOs and go after hard answers on our own. Then and only then will we collectively be in a position to deal rationally and satisfactorily with this whole space-visitor enigma.

It now appears that the enigma goes far beyond "just" space aliens and spiritual beings. There is some interaction, I believe, by a fourth, generally unknown party of ethereal intruders that we only recently are beginning to become aware of. For the most part, these beings are bizarre and unpredictable. I use the terms "ultraterrestrial" and "interdimensional" interchangeably throughout the book in referring to these strange beings.

Back in the 1920s, Charles Fort became aware of the more bizarre alien activities on this planet, although he wasn't able to put any kind of firm definition on the phenomena. He wrote some brilliant, often satirical essays and books on the subject based on the evidence available then. Charles Fort was no doubt the first ufologist. He felt that in some respects we were being "farmed" by these invisible ones. He may have been disturbingly close to a very real truth. Because Charles Fort and others may be right, it is another reason why it is so important that we—you and I—begin to deal with the ETs directly.

If you are confident that our government can represent our interests and can adequately deal with a subject as lofty as aliens from outer space better than we can, you had better think again. Our government has been actively aware of space visitors for decades and by its actions has bungled its responsibility abominably. *We* need *real* answers now!

Perhaps a part of the reason why the alien visitors have remained unseen from us, the common man, for so long is that they are waiting until we develop the technology and, perhaps, the awareness to find *them*. Is the key—the answer—really quite obvious? Will it be found only by those who exert the effort to discover it?

Sedona may be playing its own role in this drama. For some time there have been some interesting conjectures about why so many people from all parts of the world are irresistibly drawn here. A close analogy may be seen in the movie "Close Encounters of the Third Kind." There is a scene where Richard Dreyfuss is obsessed by the vague image of a stumplike mountain (Devil's Tower, Wyoming). He is a driven man. It is as if he were motivated by an outside influence to discover what his hazy mind-image meant. He and others in the movie were seeking relentlessly, until they saw pictures of Devil's Tower. Then they *knew,* and dropped everything to journey there. Dreyfuss' obsession may be similar to what is causing so many to literally drop everything, no matter where they live or what they do, and move to Sedona. They *have* to be here. I know—I am one of them.

Incidentally, "Close Encounters" may have been based on an actual event. Those of you who are old enough may recall that in the 1950s thousands of sheep and cattle were killed by an "accidental" leak of a military type of gas near Dugway Proving Grounds in Utah. It quickly cleared the area of local residents and then the area was sealed off by the military for a period of time. Did "Close Encounters" actually happen then?

Sedona is not unique to the "Close Encounters" analogy. There are a number of areas people are being drawn to—or driven to. Are these going to be the safe areas? Could it be that these untold thousands have had implants installed by a benevolent race of beings sometime in the past? Are these implantees now being called to certain localities? The reason I say a "benevolent race" is that most of the people in these groups have an urgent need to find out what is going on in a decidedly positive way. This need may come in a variety of forms, but finding the truth about it seems to be basically the same drive in each individual. When these seeking strangers meet, it is like reuniting with long-lost, loved family members; there is a definite feeling of familiarity. It may be that the entire metaphysical movement is composed of these "implantees." The implant may not necessarily be a literal object but something of a psychic, etheric, or hypnotic nature.

My connection to this sudden driving, yearning to find... something began six years ago. Events began to transpire for me then that may indeed indicate a "Close Encounter" type of implant activation. I am still not altogether comfortable with the idea of an implant, but if it is true, then I have not been harmed by it.

Prior to six years ago (1983), I had no interest whatsoever in spiritual or religious matters, UFOs or alien beings. Nor did I have clairvoyant or psychic abilities that I was aware of. One day in 1983 while living in Reno, Nevada, I was out for a walk when some force literally seized me and began steering me down the block like a robot. I turned left into a shopping center and soon found myself navigating the aisles of a bookstore. I leaned forward; automatically and without the slightest hesitation my hand went to the bottom row and pulled out a copy of *Seth Speaks* by Jane Roberts. I was instantly enthralled by the book, and consequently spent over six months studying it.

A year later I moved from Reno to Santa Cruz, California. The move began an almost fanatical obsession with anything metaphysical, occult or psychic. After settling in, I enrolled in classes at the Santa Cruz branch of the Berkeley Psychic Institute. After some elementary training, I discovered that I had an ability to see things that many people could not—even accomplished psychics. This may have nothing to do with an implant, but all of this began at approximately the same time—1983-84.

In the early stages of discovering my clairvoyant ability, I often wondered if something had gone wrong with my mind. At times I thought I had *lost* it. I experienced difficult periods of emotional and mental insecurity and severe depression. Only after years of trial and error and reassurance from other psychics, the visions I was seeing were validated and confirmed bit by bit. I now believe and trust my perceptions completely.

I have learned that I can see into human bodies. When asked, I can probe deeply into a person's deepest feelings. I can see present and past traumas. I can delve into past lives. I see imperfections or disease in a human body as black spots and dark areas. The degree of imperfections range from light grey to black—cancer is always black. I have tested these abilities hundreds of times and have found them to be accurate and reliable, although I have not learned how to recommend a remedy for a physical ailment.

Someone with a problem might call me on the phone from a thousand miles away and I can see their problem as if watching a movie, even before they tell me verbally what the problem is. I can sense and see forms of nonphysical entities, from astrals to ETs. And I can, on some basic level, communicate with these beings through pictures and thoughts, but never in words. I do, however, like many psychics, have times when nothing works. Yet there are times when my receptive senses are so elevated it is almost overpowering.

Once while attending a channeling session in Sedona, I was probing the channel psychically to see if she was on the level. I did not know the woman and she did not know me. Her name was Amritam and she was channeling a cosmic being named Oceana. Suddenly, Oceana broke off and turned to face me. I had been probing its mind and then it began probing mine with tremendous power. I've practiced this before with other psychics and it feels like tiny fingers moving and pressing around in one's mind. All was quiet for a few moments while the group watched. Then the entity Oceana remarked, to my surprise, "The reason you can see us is because you were taught how to do that on another planet." Then it turned back to the group and resumed where it had left off. I mulled that one over for some time.

I have attempted to teach clairvoyance in classes—with limited success. Everyone does indeed have psychic abilities (gifts), but in some people it does seem to be more elevated than in others. Sometimes when I am asked a question of a psychic nature, something is automatically triggered in my mind. For me it is much like watching a movie or slide show. I then relay what I see to the inquirer.

To illustrate, recently a friend called me on the phone. Their family dog had not returned home for over two days and they were getting quite upset over the dog's absence. The dog is a cherished member of the family. I paused for a moment during our conversation, and in seconds I saw in my mind an unpaved country road, to the left of which was a white house with several large shade trees surrounded by a small lawn. The house had around it a low wooden fence that extended almost to a dirt road. In the back of the house was an open field of several acres. I somehow knew that the only occupant of the house was a stocky man with graying hair. I also knew that the dog was locked in a back room of the house. The call from my friend came on a Monday. I told her that she would have the dog back in the early afternoon of the next day, Tuesday. I relayed to her what I saw in my psychic vision and instructed her to walk—not drive, as they had been doing—a quarter mile down the rural road on which they lived.

Late Tuesday morning she located a house that fit my description exactly. Standing out on the road, she called the dog's name and the dog dashed happily out from the back of the house. The dog was closely followed by a stocky man with graying hair, who said he was going to try to find the owner—eventually. I have now done this same sort of thing dozens of times.

Six weeks ago I was asked to do a clairvoyant reading for a woman from Indiana. Normally I want to know what a person wants in a reading before I will do it, as there are some areas I choose to stay out of. But in this case she was referred by a friend of mine and the Indiana woman would not be available until the night of the reading. It turned out the Indiana woman was rather distraught over the recent murders of two of her friends in Florida. They had been an attractive young couple in their late twenties. She wanted to know if I could give her some details of the murders. The murders were drug-related and what little she knew about them was disturbing. The police, mysteriously, would not actively pursue this case. As a rule, I would have turned this sort of thing down, but out of curiosity I went ahead with it. I told her what I saw psychically in connection with the murders; it took about an hour. She said little, paid me and left.

Two weeks later I got a call that three people from Florida urgently wanted an appointment with me for a further reading in connection with the murders. I wondered at that point if I might be getting in too deeply. I agreed to the meeting and the trio flew from Florida to Arizona for one afternoon session. They were in Sedona only that afternoon and left early the next morning. During the four-hour session I gave them names, a description of who had been present, guns that had been involved, accomplices, descriptions of cars, a license plate number, interiors and exteriors of houses, what the murderer did for a legitimate living, the country he was originally from and a lot more. They said it all fit perfectly.

At the end of the long, exhausting reading they brought out a tape and said that I should hear it. It was a hot day—over 100 degrees. As I listened to the tape, even though I was tired and perspiring, chills ran up and down my body at what I was hearing. It was a tape that had been recorded two months prior to that Saturday reading. The reading had been done by a woman who was a professional psychic in North Carolina—also about this double murder. And it was word for word what I had moments before told them! Even the odd phrases I had used in certain descriptions were identical to those on the two-month-old tape. The psychic in North Carolina and I both advised the three to stay out of it, or very likely the same thing would happen to them.

I only mention these psychic abilities because it may be that I have a clearer vision or insight than some ufologists into certain areas. As a result, perhaps I am more accurate than some regarding phenomena such as nonphysical beings and UFOs. I am not a professional psychic/clairvoyant, nor do I have aspirations of becoming one. There are three areas I stay out of under any circumstance: money matters, romantic relationships, and the future. If the psychic abilities I have are somehow unique, I have dedicated myself and these abilities to finding solutions that will benefit all. By doing so, I get answers to my own questions.

CHAPTER 3

Men in Black and Black Helicopters

Black helicopters and "men in black" have made their presence known on a number of occasions in the Sedona area. Among prominent UFO researchers in this country, the opinion seems to be split as to whether men in black and black helicopters are U.S. military, space alien, or both. My position is that it is a mixture of both alien and military. Men in black have, since the sixties, come to be called "MIBs" in UFO circles.

Often after a UFO flap or during a long series of UFO sightings, MIBs and black helicopters show up at the same time. The more serious the UFO activity, the more blatant the MIB/black helicopter activity. From the military standpoint, the use of MIBs and black helicopters seems to be directed toward frightening and intimidating UFO witnesses and researchers. On the alien side of the coin, the use of black helicopters seems to be one of camouflage. In many close sightings around the world, helicopters have been seen to transform into UFOs. Conversely, UFOs have been seen rematerializing into the configuration of a helicopter. During the years when cattle mutilations were at their peak over most of the western states, black unmarked helicopters were often seen in the vicinity shortly before, during or after a mutilation. (Incidentally, in the last twenty-five years there have been well over 10,000 cattle mutilations, primarily in the western United States. The perpetrators have never been caught. The government is *still* calling it a hoax—or the work of a satanic cult group.)

Strange helicopters have also been observed at close range that are completely silent in the air. I can attest to that because I saw one. I observed a helicopter directly overhead late one evening as I was walking in Oak Creek Canyon. The flying object had the configuration of a very large helicopter, yet it made no sound whatsoever. I estimated its distance at three to five hundred yards from where I stood. It had a pulsing red light on the bottom of the ship and a steady white light at each end.

Near Sedona recently there has been a bizarre but short-lived rash of black helicopter/MIB experiences. All of this activity has been centered in the Fay, Red, Boynton and Long Canyon areas. These four canyons are close to one another. Most of the activity has taken place near the mouth of Long Canyon. Several major developments and properties in that general area have fallen into bankruptcy in the past, whereas developments elsewhere in Sedona have prospered. It is, and has been, openly speculated in Sedona that "something" doesn't want major developments in the canyonlands.

What has been occurring in that general location in the way of extraordinary phenomena is one of the greatest mysteries I have ever encountered. MIBs and black helicopters are only a small part of it.

Here are some of the MIB/black helicopter occurrences in this area. Seven months ago (spring 1989) prospective buyers were looking over a property when two black helicopters suddenly flew out of Long Canyon. One black helicopter came within a hundred yards of these buyers. The lead helicopter tipped forward menacingly and remained in that position for five minutes. Then both helicopters backed off about a quarter of a mile, where they remained stationary for approximately twenty minutes. These black helicopters were of the type commonly written about in UFO encounter reports. It should be noted that some military helicopters are standardly painted a flat black. However, they have obvious identifying insignia and clear windows. What makes the black helicopters in UFO flaps different is that the windows are always as dark as the fuselage, and there are no registration numbers nor identifying markings whatsoever.

The helicopter experience that the two buyers had, also happened to Art Mossberg, a Michigan UFO researcher. After the forward-tipped helicopter departed, Mossberg discovered to his horror that his pacemaker had stopped. His doctor later confirmed that there was extensive tissue damage in Mossberg's chest caused by some type of unidentifiable radiation. Whether the two buyers were exposed to radiation is uncertain, although one of the gentlemen remarked that for several days after the incident he was "not quite himself."

Another misfortune that befell the prospective buyers came when one of the men had a steering wheel lock up in his hands, resulting in the wreckage of a very expensive automobile. Several weeks after that a woman reported a similar incident only a mile from the earlier crash. Both cars were totaled, but the drivers were uninjured. A third similar crash occurred when a four-wheel-drive vehicle rolled over on nearby Dry Creek Road. The driver simply shrugs his shoulders when he tries to explain the accident. He says there is no logical reason for the strange incident. It was almost as if his vehicle were swept off the road.

I have made inquiries, and have been told that military helicopters are forbidden by law to fly at low altitudes over National Forest Wilderness areas. Ten air miles to the north of Sedona is the Navajo Army Depot, a sprawling munitions storage area five miles across—plenty of room to berth an aircraft with the limited range of a helicopter. Most unmarked black helicopters are reported to be of the Vietnam UH-1 Huey type. The UH-60 Sikorsky Black Hawk has also been reported.

In the area of Long Canyon I investigated a "man in black" (MIB) incident reported by a man who had been camping in the desert until he could afford a room in town. He said that one morning he awoke at dawn and, to his mounting fright, realized he was watching a small force of heavily armed men searching for something in the thick pine, juniper and manzanita forest. They were so intent in their search they had not noticed him. The camper hid in a manzanita bush. He said the armed men were wearing dark uniforms without insignia. The armed men moved on to the north, and the camper beat a hasty retreat out of the area.

At about the time of that episode, a woman with whom I am acquainted and whose integrity I can unhesitatingly vouch for, observed a disk-shaped UFO with clearly visible windows pass silently over her car as she drove past the mouth of Fay Canyon. Minutes after, she sighted an entirely black helicopter near the back of Fay Canyon moving in a distinct search pattern. She watched the helicopter for ten minutes until it went over the summit of Bear Mountain.

I talked to a man (I will call him Phil) who lives in the vicinity of the four-canyon area. His experience may be indirectly connected with the others. He related to me that he was paid an unexpected visit one night by two men. One of the men—six feet tall, dark brown hair, medium build and in his late twenties—identified himself as a CIA agent. According to Phil, the "agent's" identification badge (or card) seemed entirely authentic and in order. Phil was suspicious of their motives. He thought the visit might have something to do with the rather dramatic UFO sightings he had been having at the time. The interview was conducted formally, rather mundanely and nothing unusual was asked. But when the "agents" got up to leave, the "CIA" man turned to Phil and told him, in effect, that if Phil didn't keep his nose out of places it shouldn't be, Phil wouldn't be around to see the next month. The CIA has flatly denied having a man in the area at that time. I have talked to retired military intelligence agents and they have told me confidentially that the CIA is indeed very much interested in what goes on in and around Sedona concerning UFOs.

Back in the 1970s a Maine doctor, who was working on the case of a local UFO landing, had a strange visitor in his locked office late one night. The doctor heard a muffled sound in his outer office, and as he looked up, a man dressed in black walked silently in. The intruder had makeup awkwardly applied to his face, masklike, as if he were trying to look human. The stranger reached out his arm and directed the doctor to put a coin in his hand. The doctor pulled a quarter from his pocket and put it in the man's hand. In seconds the coin began to glow bright blue, and in less than a minute it vanished entirely. The visitor warned the doctor that if he did not drop his UFO investigation, his heart would disappear in the same way the coin did. The phantomlike visitor turned and went out as silently as he had come in.

A California woman I interviewed told me of a man-in-black encounter. Two years ago she was driving in the mountains when, due to a moment of carelessness, her car went off the road and got stuck in deep sand. She stepped out of the car to size up the situation. As she did, she heard the sound of a car coming up the road behind her. Around the corner came a gleaming automobile, which somehow seemed too big and somehow not proportioned exactly right. It drew up alongside her mired car. She told how the doors of the big car opened simultaneously and four oriental-looking men, dressed all in black, got out. One of them inquired if she needed help. She replied that she did, and in minutes they had her car back on the road. She told me this all happened so fast she barely had time to react. She exclaimed to me that the weirdest thing about it all was that it was a hot, summer day—and all four men were wearing heavy winter coats! This same woman has had previous abduction experiences in California; and I suspect this incident was directly related to them.

As the last entry in this chapter, I will relate what has been the strangest incident of all concerning the MIB/black aircraft phenomenon in Sedona. A driver with one of the jeep-tour companies here in Sedona called me one night (as I was working on this book) and related the following incident. It seems he and four passengers were in his jeep on a tour of a scenic area overlooking Long Canyon. They had stopped to admire the view on Dry Creek Road (the Vultee Arch-Dry Creek section) when they noticed a twin-engine aircraft banking toward them. As it came closer they saw that it wasn't a normal airplane at all. It approached to within better viewing range, and they saw that the plane was entirely black; the windows were as black as the fuselage. (These are called "phantoms" among UFO researchers.) Among the people in the tour group was an experienced pilot, who remarked that he had never seen a plane like it. As the plane flew by them, they saw that it had no registration numbers nor any type of insignia. The pilot in the group said that because of the banking angle, the plane did not have enough air speed to keep it aloft. However, it did stay aloft! As it passed directly in front of them, no part of the plane reflected sunlight. They said that strangest of all was the fact that it looked like a plane within a plane. It seemed to have a double fuselage—almost like a mirage within a mirage.

CHAPTER 4

The UFO/Military Base in Boynton Canyon

When I first arrived in Sedona, one of the first unusual stories I heard was that of a UFO/military base underground in Boynton Canyon. Being a devout skeptic and usually the last one to be convinced of something until I experience it myself, I relegated this "base" rumor to the too-far-out category. But I do have a burning curiosity, and the very idea of a UFO base in that area intrigued me no end. I continued to hear variations of the underground-base rumors, along with some stories too wild to repeat here. Still the story persisted and, as they say, where there is smoke there is fire.

I followed the details of the rumors closely, particularly when a few individuals with whom I am acquainted and whom I consider to be of high character, intelligence and common sense, gave high credence to the possibility of an underground base. Events and experiences began to add up and I began to take the stories more seriously, even if most of it didn't make a whole lot of sense. As I mentioned previously, this has now turned out to be part of one of the greatest mysteries that I have ever encountered. And I am nowhere near the bottom of it yet.

The turning point concerning the Boynton base rumors came for me one night in July 1988. One quiet, moon-filled summer night, I had walked up to the saddle (a rocky promontory overlooking the entrance to Boynton Canyon) to meditate in a popular local vortex. I had spent about an hour in meditation when I began to be aware of something distinctly out of place. It was a sound. I stood up and walked to the middle of the saddle, where the sound seemed to be more pronounced. As I stood there I could hear a barely audible humming sound, like that of a huge engine running. I quickly discovered that not only was I hearing the sound, but I was feeling the vibrations associated with the sound beneath my feet. The ground under my feet was literally vibrating. When I placed both hands on the rocky ground I could feel the vibration through my hands as well.

I began to run through my mind some of the stories I had heard about the supposed underground base. But it all seemed crazy—why would the CIA, or whomever, put an underground base near a developing city like Sedona? But I knew that here somewhere underground, an engine was running at a moderate speed. An engine that must have been *at least* in the several-thousand-horsepower range. I have worked as a welder/mechanic and have an extensive knowledge of large and small engines, so I am a fair judge of an engine's size.

As I stood there I mulled over some of the base stories that I had been hearing over the previous two years. One of the first was that when the new road into Boynton Canyon was being built, an Indian burial ground was bulldozed in the process. The bones, I understand, were not ceremoniously disposed of. I talked to a man who worked on the road crew at the time. He said that right after the incident all sorts of things began to go wrong with the project. For weeks afterward strange breakdowns and almost supernatural problems occurred—then stopped abruptly. Maybe this doesn't have anything to do with the underground-base theory and the vibrations, but then again maybe somehow it does.

In 1985 there were reliable reports of single military vehicles as well as convoys of large, military-type trucks entering Boynton Canyon in the wee hours. I interviewed a woman who said that in 1985 she had followed a huge ten-wheeled olive-drab military truck as it rumbled through Sedona at 2:00 a.m. It turned off the highway and headed toward Boynton. She followed it for awhile but broke off the pursuit after a few miles. There is no logical or practical reason why any big military truck should for any reason—at *any* time—be in that area.

UFOs have often been seen coming and going from Boynton Canyon. A Pennsylvania woman told me that in 1986, she was sitting on the trunk of her car at 11:00 p.m. waiting for friends to come down from the saddle, when suddenly three brightly lit

UFOs flew by at low altitude. She said that within five minutes two of the UFOs returned and disappeared back into the Canyon.

Also in 1985 a construction worker who was working on the new road decided to go for a walk into Boynton Canyon on his lunch hour. He had gone only a short distance into the canyon when several hundred feet ahead he heard a sound similar to that of a helicopter taking off. The sound grew to a roar, and a huge donut-shaped dust cloud began to billow up around the sound. He said that he saw nothing but trees, cactus, rocks and dust—yet there was an enormous, invisible object lifting off in front of him. The round dust cloud billowed larger and larger as the thing rose higher and higher. Then the helicopter sound faded gradually into the distance over the red rocks.

Since my initial cataloging of unusual events involving the five canyons—Red, Fay, Boynton, Long and Secret Canyons—I have come to the conclusion that whatever it is that is going on is not centered in Boynton Canyon, as many believe. The center of the activity is farther to the north on or near Secret Mountain, which is about two air miles from Boynton. I have recorded dozens of paranormal experiences and reports, both minor and major, put them all together, and Secret Mountain seems to be the source of all this extraordinary activity. If there is indeed some sort of "base," I think Secret Mountain is where it is located.

Even as I write, UFO stories are coming in. The following incident happened only last week as I was doing the final rewrite of this book. There were two men camping at the Long Canyon trailhead. "Don" and "Joe" had returned to their camp one night at 3:00 a.m. When they were within a quarter mile of their camp, they saw extremely bright flashes of blue light reflecting on the hood of their car from the sky above. Moments later a UFO flew into their field of vision. The two men said that the UFO was a glowing white color and had what looked to be about six portholes or windows. They arrived at their campsite a bit disturbed at the sighting. Don, a heavy smoker, found that he was out of cigarettes. After a small debate about the wisdom of it, he decided to drive into town to buy more cigarettes.

Joe stayed at camp, although reluctantly, for he was extremely tired and needed sleep. As Don departed for town, Joe crawled into his sleeping bag. Minutes later, he heard a sound like that of a high wind—then it stopped as quickly as it had begun. Joe, now wide awake, heard the unexpected sound of footsteps on both sides of his tent. I asked him if it might have been deer or wild pigs, but he said no, that whatever they were, they walked on two legs. At that point, his voice breaking with emotion, he told me that the tent flaps on his small tent opened. In the opening was a face that terrified him. It had enormous, round piercing eyes surrounded by wrinkled, reptilian-looking skin.

He remembers nothing more from that point until his friend returned. Little was said of the incident until the next day, when Don, the smoker, developed a strange nosebleed high in his left nostril. One week later Joe, who had remained behind, developed an identical nosebleed. What had happened to these two men? We will discuss further examples of this kind of activity later.

When doing this research, I take into account numerous and varied paranormal incidents from different people who, in most cases, do not know each other and do not live in the same location. When two or more stories turn out to be fundamentally the same—odd as they may seem—there is often a resulting corroboration of events pointing to something very much out of the ordinary. What was thought to be unique to the Boynton Canyon area in reality occurs over the general five-canyon area near Sedona. The vibrating sound I heard and felt has been experienced by individuals in Boynton, Long and Secret Canyons.

In the spring of 1989 a local couple, well-known Sedona residents, were camping in Secret Canyon. After they had turned in for the night, they were suddenly aware of a strange vibrating sound that seemed to emanate from the ground. In this instance, the sound grew to such a volume that it was impossible to sleep. They were so close to the source of the sound that they could hear and feel it very clearly. The man described the steady humming as having a consistent oscillating, wavering tone. It was too far to walk to their car at night, so, having no choice, they remained sleepless until dawn, when the sound gradually abated. They walked to their car without further incident.

Secret Canyon has a very otherworldly feeling to it, similar to walking through a haunted house. In the past three years I have spoken to only one person who has hiked or camped in Secret Canyon and who said they felt comfortable there. It is a very strange place.

In April 1988 about 10:00 p.m., a local man was looking toward Secret Canyon through Soldier's Pass. He observed two small, bright lights, which he first thought were airplane headlights. He watched them carefully for a few minutes but saw that they did not change in size or intensity. He concluded that they were merely stars and started to turn away. Suddenly, the two lights began to shoot blazing shafts of light down into the canyons far below. The spectacle lasted only a few seconds. He shrugged it off as some sort of explainable aberration of the atmosphere. He found out differently two days later when he was having breakfast at a local restaurant. A friend who knew about his sighting called him over and introduced him to two young women who had been camping that night in Secret Canyon. The two women told him that they had also seen the lights, which had been positioned directly above them in the night sky. The young women said that due to the fantastic, unexplainable and intermittent actions of the lights, they had spent a terror-filled and sleepless night in the canyon.

An older gentleman who lives in the Long Canyon area states that on more than one occasion he has been awakened at night by the rumbling sound of a convoy of large, heavy trucks passing near his house on their way into the canyons. If you are acquainted with that area, you will know that there is nowhere that a convoy of heavy trucks could go and not be seen by someone, somewhere. Curiously, however, many individuals at different times have heard these seemingly phantom convoys. What are they? Where are they going? What are they up to? I have learned that this anomalous sound has been heard at different sites around the country and the world. And, perhaps not unexpectedly, it always happens in areas where there has been recent ongoing UFO activity.

All of this indicates the presence of a very real mystery. It is unlikely that an underground base exists in Boynton Canyon, but the possibility or probability of an underground "base" in the area of Secret Canyon and Secret Mountain, in my opinion, is very high.

Another last-minute (April 1990) followup to this chapter is an incident I recently learned of: An individual was hiking in a remote canyon near Secret Mountain and discovered a pile of steel crates. On them was stamped the words "U.S. Dept. of Commerce."

Several weeks later, by sheer chance, I talked to another person who gave me some further information relative to the discovery of the crates. It seems there was a woman who met a man here in Sedona and they dated briefly. During this time the man told her that he was working in the Sedona area and was employed by the Dept. of Commerce. He/they were building test vehicles that can *run without air*. Run without air? (Underground, perhaps?) Department of Commerce?

The girl broke off the dating, as she decided the fellow was a bit strange. He left town several weeks later. After he left, the woman began to act uncharacteristically. Normally cheerful and outgoing, she became withdrawn and was described by friends as apparently being under extreme stress. Shortly after, she dissolved, for a pittance, a thriving business she owned and left town with hardly a word to anyone. The obvious question is—why? Did she perhaps come across some sort of information that was too frightening to deal with?

CHAPTER 5

The Burned Tree

The subject of UFOs and alien beings on Earth is bound to be a controversial one no matter who engages in the subject. Scorn, ridicule and disbelief have long been a Pavlovian response for many. The news media and various government agencies are the source of much of the ridicule. To further complicate matters, there have been many elaborate hoaxes down through the years that have led responsible researchers down a sometimes embarrassing and humiliating road. Journalists especially cannot afford this kind of mistake. Ultimately, hoaxes of any kind severely hamper serious UFO research by dedicated investigators.

To further compound matters, there is an ongoing disinformation campaign by the government. It is leaking fake documents, rumors of landings, crashes, alien activity, etc., and this creates even more confusion in the UFO research community. Going still further, it may well be that there are invisible/interdimensional pranksters at work—as if we didn't have enough to deal with already. Ever since I read Robert Anton Wilson's provocative book, *Cosmic Trigger*, fifteen years ago, I have deliberated long over the possible existence of these beings. Circumstantial evidence points time and time again to the real presence of these phantasmagorical meddlers. Wilson called them the "Illuminati," and proceeded to build an excellent case to substantiate his theory. The term "illuminati" is not new; it came into existence in the Middle Ages and is closely linked to semisecret groups such as the Masons.

These unseen pranksters seem capable of weaving incredible riddles that involve any and all of us. For example, there is the story of a local man. When he was a boy out delivering newspapers —on a Friday the 13th—he was hit by a 13-year-old Dodge Dart. Both of his legs were broken. The house number of the property he landed on was 814—which adds up to 13. The ambulance that came for him was from Fire Station No. 13. He was put in bed number 13 in the hospital, but was later moved to room 418 — 4 + 1 + 8 = 13. His mother noticed that the traction weights on his legs weighed 13 pounds. He had 13 stitches in his right leg, where they had to put a 13-inch pin. Both this man's name and that of the driver added together equalled—yes, 13!

Mere coincidence? I don't think so. This sort of thing has been happening to Robert Anton Wilson all of his life. Wilson's number is 23. It seems almost everything he does somehow adds up to 23. Wilson is gifted with exceptional intelligence, which has enabled him to make sense out of his drama with the number 23.

Is there in fact some etheric agency out there who is at times playing tricks on us? Perhaps if we, like Wilson, had the time and patience to figure it out and add up all of our coincidences, we could understand what is behind it all and benefit from it. The above occurrence happens at one time or another to everyone. But how often do we pay attention to something like that, something that may be of considerable significance in the long run?

This book is filled with this kind of riddle, only they don't add up to a number—they add up to an event. The answer to that riddle is one I am determined to discover!

Long Canyon is in the center of an area encompassing perhaps twenty square miles. This general area has been the scene of many extraordinary paranormal events that may seem unrelated, but somehow they are connected. They constitute part of the riddle that I have been dealing with in the following incident, that of the "burned tree."

I have spent a large portion of my time tracking rumors and stories down to their source. The burned-tree incident is one of them. I encountered many dead ends, or trails that evaporated, during my research. But some trails turned out to be worth every bit of my effort to follow them. The burned-tree story, as I originally heard it, was that someone had photographs of a tree that had been set on fire, ostensibly by a UFO. I was particularly skeptical of this one, because during thunderstorms here we get a lot of lightning strikes. This area has some of the most intense electrical storm activity in the world. It seemed to me that someone had seen a burning tree that had been struck by lightning and then somehow connected it to a UFO. It is disturbing how an event can get blown totally out of proportion each time it is retold. Sometimes by the fifth or sixth person, you get a story so radically different that it doesn't even vaguely resemble the actual, rather simple event. It was beginning to look like the burned-tree story fell into that category.

During my interviewing I located a man who said that there indeed existed a tree that had mysteriously burned, and that there had been a white-hot-appearing UFO sighted by several witnesses that same day. This occurred on the afternoon of July 23, 1988. I was given directions, and after a short hike located the mysterious tree. I saw that it was indeed rather unusual, so I snapped several photographs of it. The day was July 24, 1989—a year and a day after the tree had burned.

The tree was an Arizona cypress that was actually eight trees in one, for it had eight trunks growing out of one base, the entire growth in the shape of a funnel. After taking pictures of the tree, I concluded that it looked like a lightning strike, as unusual as it was. The tree had burned at the base and the trunks had fallen away from the center—odd, but certainly not impossible. But then upon strolling around the area, I found and photographed three other trees that were flattened in the same strange manner. These other three trees, however, had not been burned. It was as if some enormous weight, or force field, had settled upon them.

I thought deeply about this newest addition to the Sedona Mystery. In the canyons there are trees of all sizes broken in ways that are not easily attributable to natural forces. Ask any hiker who regularly hikes deep into the canyons, and many of them will have their own mysterious broken-tree story.

Far back in Long Canyon there is a place where trees are sequentially broken off as if an object had come down at a sharp angle with great force. One can stand at the bottom tree and sight up to the top tree. There is a clear angle of descent by following the broken trees, from the shortest to the tallest break.

I went back to talk to the man who had given me directions to the tree. As it turned out, he was the mystery man who had taken the original photographs of the tree and had also seen the UFO near the burned tree on July 23. He related to me how that night there had been an eerie phosphorescent radiance rising from the location of the tree. He said people who were in the area were very frightened by this spectacle. I have confirmed this through other sources. He took six photographs of the tree the day after it burned. I was amazed at what they showed.

I saw that the tree had been a *living* tree and had been completely burned to ashes at its very base—not the trunks or limbs, only the base. As he was walking toward it taking pictures, a reddish-yellow glow began to appear sequentially in the pictures. The last three photos have two brilliant orbs of reddish-yellow light in each of them. It was as if something had seen him taking the pictures and had come down to see what he was doing.

The camera he used is an expensive, professional model and not prone to producing defective photographs. He later told me somewhat guardedly that that day the ground around the tree had been watersoaked—but it hadn't rained in weeks; the woods that day were tinder dry!

The only conclusion one could make, if the evidence is indeed accurate, is that a glowing, flying object had either deliberately or inadvertently set the living tree on fire and then dropped water or some other liquid on it to put it out. Another piece to a big puzzle.

CHAPTER 6

The Abduction of Frank Ramsey

I find the whole subject of UFOs and ETs, as well as anything connected to that subject, to be absolutely fascinating—even some of the attributes of the phenomenon viewed by some with a measure of fear and loathing, or even terror. I think the reason for the fear is, in part, that many people fail entirely to grasp the actual magnitude of the presence of alien beings here on our planet.

I feel that the existence alone of these ET entities, as well as the almost inconceivable technology and mental abilities they must possess, is an opportunity for us to learn from them. It is a chance for us to break away finally from the railroad-tracklike rut we have been in for so long. Look, for example, at some of our social, economic and religious belief patterns. Some, if not all of them, should have been tossed in the junk pile decades ago. Worst of all, like obedient sheep, the common man has been manipulated into position by greedy and power-hungry individuals for thousands of years.

This is a good chance to make a new start—a clean, fresh start. Will it take something like bizarre-looking space aliens to jolt humanity out of our subservient, materialistic lethargy? Humanity surely needs to begin to work cooperatively together to create heaven on Earth and to preserve what was given us to cherish.

The abduction of Frank Ramsey is a prime example of a worst-case scenario. He was taken against his will, examined on a ship and left with a feeling of having been personally violated. He was abused and dumped back on the planet with no consciously remembered reason why this was done to him. Frank has been abducted several times in the past, and after the first incident he nearly had to be hospitalized because of resulting emotional trauma. On this particular occasion, Frank remembered some of what had happened to him. At that time there were no support groups for abductees, although now there are many. These abductions by aliens not only of Frank but of countless others are absolutely real. We need to know *why* they are doing it. We need the explanation from the aliens themselves. We need concrete answers from the source of this activity and from *no one else!*

Here is Frank Ramsey's story in his own words. "It was April in 1976. I was staying at the. . .Ranch near Loy Butte. I was out for a walk late one afternoon and I had gone out to the end of the ranch road to take pictures of the sunset. I took the pictures and had turned to go back. By the way, I had the exact same flashlight with me that I had had in the other incident—not just the same model, but the exact same flashlight. [Author's note: This referred to a previous abduction in the same general area years earlier.] I turned to walk down this road that went around the other end of the ranch. I did that to avoid going back through the rocks and boulders the way I had come. But something compelled me to continue walking down the road past the ranch. Well, I was aware that it was 'something' compelling me. But out of curiosity, I let 'it' do it. So I went ahead and walked.

"In a while I came to a crossroads. Puzzled by where this other road went that I didn't even know about, I made a pile of rocks at the edge of this old road. I figured that the next day I could drive around, rediscover that old road and follow it. Just then the whole place lit up like daylight. I looked above me and there was a bright white sphere probably 30 to 40 feet off the ground. I ducked into a bush and reloaded my camera. I was determined to get a picture this time.

"This thing took off—it would flash like a huge, brilliant flashbulb, and then it would be gone. And then a split second later it would flash fifty or sixty miles away. And then it would come back. And it did it again and again! Back and forth! Well, I took off through the bushes—not on the road. I did not turn on my flashlight this time. In the dark I worked my way back almost to the ranch. I saw the sphere once with its light very dim, going along a wash behind me. So I figured it could do just about anything. But I was still trying to get back to the ranch.

"I almost got back. I was near the south end of the ranch, working my way down a wash in the dark. There was no moon to speak of; it was somewhat overcast, which didn't help any. It was then that I saw someone standing out on the side of a hill, waving a light at me. Well, I assumed this was one of my friends from the ranch; there were three of us that lived there. And so I turned my light on to answer. And I hollered to the person on the hillside and began to move toward him.

"Well, just about that time a car stopped on the road, the main road on the ridge above the ranch. Two people got out of the car, a man and a woman, and they began yelling and honking the car's horn. Then I realized that these were my friends from the ranch. I thought, well...I remember the exact thought: 'Well! If that's Laura and Paul up there, then *what's this!!*' I turned to look, and as I strained my vision it became clear to me that there was a sphere on the ground. It was the same one as before and it had a door open. I could make out a muted light inside. The thing was by then only about a hundred feet away—I had walked a long way toward it. My heart started to race when I saw that there was a human-shaped creature standing by the side of the opening. This creature was made up of white light. I turned to run and the only thing I know to say is that it was like a 'freeze frame.' The next thing I know, everything's different. I'm standing on a rock. I don't know where I am. The only memory I have after turning to run was of being in the air about four or five feet above a big bush with my camera, tripod and all. I was like in a picture. It was, again, like a freeze frame. I was totally immobile; I couldn't move.

"Anyway, here I am standing on this rock and my first thought was to see if I was all there. I thought I might be hurt. I checked to see if my camera was intact and still with me—and my tripod. I looked to see if I was all torn up and bleeding from running through the cactus, and my socks all full of thorns. None of this was true! I was just fine! I wasn't cut and scratched like I should have been, running through the bushes. I was very clean. I had all my camera gear with me. But I did not know where I was. I finally figured out that I was standing to the north of the ranch because I heard dogs barking. I turned and walked toward the dogs. It turned out they were at another ranch, and I was a long way from where I had been last. A mile and a half, probably—maybe as much as two miles from where I had been. I wandered around in the darkness for some time. Finally, I saw the vague outline of Loy Butte silhouetted against the sky. It was then that I knew I was going in the wrong direction! Having hiked the area, I was somewhat familiar with the terrain. I got the right direction and managed to work my way back to the ranch. I must have wandered around for a couple of hours. I really don't know because I was so disoriented. But it was at least a couple of hours.

"Back at the ranch I told my story to my friends. I am not sure they believed me, but they did remember seeing my flashlight from the roadway where they were. Anyway, I have a memory of being inside that sphere. I remember looking out of a porthole-type window and I remember seeing stars outside it. I didn't remember anything else." [Note: After the incident, bit by bit, he began to remember the creatures. They were the Whitley Strieber type, with oversized, bulbous heads, no ears, no hair, large almond eyes, etc.]

"I don't know why these incidents have occurred to me—why me? If it ever happens again, I am going to face it without fear and without terror. And with solidity of purpose, I will find out what is going on. I will not let myself be overcome again!!"

*

After reading Frank's account of his abduction, you may be left feeling somewhat stirred up. I was. You have to wonder if perhaps something like that happened to you and you don't remember it. Maybe it has. Few people have a conscious memory of an alien abduction. When lots of people get really riled up, it is then that we will get some solid answers. Frank's case (and there are now hundreds of similar, documented ones) is rather unusual because he does have memory of events leading up to his abduction. He also has some recollection of the abduction itself.

In Frank's experience, the abductors were very sloppy in their handling of the abduction. Usually they are not. In the majority of cases there is only strangely missing time. Typically, the abductee is going from point A to point B, which would normally take, say, ten minutes. The perplexed individual then discovers, to his or her consternation, that the trip actually took *two hours* and ten minutes! What happened during those missing hours? Has it happened before? Will it happen again?

Most abductions in the last ten or twenty years were from the individual's own bedroom in the early hours of the morning, instead of from a car, a boat or during a camping, fishing, or hunting trip, etc. Why the recent shift? Might it be that alien methods or technology in that area have become more efficient? What are these abductors up to? Are these abductions for our welfare or for theirs? It's probably more for our welfare and our planet than for theirs—in the long run. But only they know the exact reason why!

Regardless, these nocturnal intrusions *must* stop! It is our right to know the reason for such intrusions. The few ET races that are presently doing this should come to us, not the government, face to face and explain what they are doing and why they are doing it. Then we can *choose* to cooperate with them in these activities if their reasons are convincing and appropriate.

CHAPTER 7

Two Strange Canyon Entities

I am thoroughly convinced that we are being visited on a continual basis by curious and, for the most part, friendly, nonphysical entities, but from another *dimension*. I believe they differ from space ETs, astrals or spiritual beings by the mode of their operation. These entities are not physical as we know physical, and they probably never have been. Perhaps there are two avenues of evolution—physical and nonphysical—and they long ago chose the latter. These I mentioned in chapter two as the fourth level of entities—interdimensionals, or ultraterrestrials.

There are areas in the depths of at least three of Sedona's canyons where these beings can sometimes be found. I have now been to one of these spots 20 or 30 times to experience this particular phenomenon, which seems to be resident there. I have taken a number of individuals along to test their reaction. They have generally confirmed my own. Especially on the occasion when I invited world UFO lecturer and retired military intelligence officer Virgil Armstrong to come along. More on that later in this chapter.

I am quite certain that there is still another type of creature, a lower form of evolving life, which accesses the same pathways that advanced interdimensional/ultraterrestrial beings use. I believe these "lower" creatures *may be* entirely physical. Somehow they have the ability or know-how to use these same interdimensional pathways the advanced beings use.

I will illustrate my theory about the "lower" interdimensional life forms first. Down through history there are the stories of monsters or unusual creatures that appear, stay around for awhile and are seen by hundreds, sometimes thousands of people—and then vanish. Most of these creatures or beasts seem to have a mentality not much higher than that of an animal. Almost all of them leave physical traces of some sort, which more or less proves they weren't the product of a fertile imagination or someone's fanciful boredom.

A multitude of books have been written on the subject of the appearances of these types of creatures. Take, for example, these next two cases, which are just two of thousands in history. One occurred in Illinois and one in South Carolina. Nineteen years ago the Illinois papers were full of reports of the sightings of upright-walking catlike creatures. These creatures had been reported in 38 sightings all over Illinois by a cross-section of residents, young and old. They left lots of unidentifiable catlike tracks. The sightings of these creatures scared the wits out of dozens of unsuspecting people, including a few law-enforcement officers. Not your usual down-on-the-farm Saturday night fare.

During the height of the cat-creature appearances, one of the weirdest incidents happened at the southern tip of Illinois in Alexander County. On Friday, April 10, 1970, Lew Cates of Cairo was driving on State Route 3 to Olive Branch, Illinois, to pick up his wife. About 8:30 p.m., a mile south of Olive Branch on this dark, mostly deserted road that parallels the edge of Shawnee National Forest, Cates' car suddenly quit running.

Cates got out of the car and went around to raise the hood. He heard a noise to his left, turned, and was shocked to see two quarter-sized, almond-shaped, greenish glowing eyes staring *down* at him! Before he had a chance to react, the six-foot-tall black form jumped him. It hit him hard in the face with two large, padded feet and they both went down. It kept Cates pinned to the pavement. As they rolled around, the creature shredded Cates' shirt and inflicted wounds to his chest, shoulders and abdomen with two-inch claws. Cates desperately held the creature's mouth open at locked arm's length. He was certain that it was trying for his throat. He saw that it had long, yellow cat fangs.

Cates couldn't see the creature's features very well, but as they fought on the pavement, he grabbed handfuls of thick fur, which felt like steel wool. The creature was dry but had a strong, wet animal smell to it. The creature also growled low, rumbling growls like nothing he had heard before. A diesel truck appeared and roared past them. The sudden appearance of the big truck frightened the creature. It leaped up and bolted across the road, fading into the darkness.

Cates got up, went to his car and found that it started normally. (This is identical to what UFO abductees report.) The truck driver, John Pendleton, was waiting for Cates in Olive Branch and flagged him down. Pendleton declared he was unable to stop his truck to help. He said he got a good look at the catlike creature that was wrestling with Cates on the pavement. Cates was treated at St. Mary's Hospital in Cairo and released the same day.

During the time of Cates encounter, other separate encounters with strange, catlike creatures were reported from one end of Illinois to the other. From the descriptions there seemed to be at least four distinctly different cat species roaming Illinois. Their sizes varied and their weights ranged from an estimated 20 to 30 pounds to over 500. The tracks they left were examined by experts and the conclusion was that they were like nothing ever seen before.

Then, as always, as abruptly as the sightings began, they stopped. It was as if they had come and gone through a portal in space—and maybe they did! These odd appearances always follow the same general pattern of a sudden appearance and later disappearance, no matter where in the world they occur. Cates' account is unique in that it is extremely rare for one of these creatures to physically attack a human being. This, as in UFO encounters, demands a rational explanation. If these creatures are indeed coming through windows or portals, what else is out there?

A more recent incident occurred in 1988. In Lee County, South Carolina, there was a rash of "lizard man" sightings. Most of the sightings were in Scape Ore Swamp. These incidents abruptly ended after State Trooper Joseph Hanson and Lee County Deputy Willis Rand went to investigate a report of overturned barrels near Bramlett Road. The two policemen checked the area and found nothing unusual. They drove away, but on a hunch turned around after a few minutes and went back to the site to take another look.

They immediately noticed a broken tree limb nine feet off the ground that had not been broken before. Then the two men were shocked to discover fresh, fourteen-inch-long, clawed, three-toed tracks. These tracks were seven inches wide at the ball of the foot and were imbedded one inch into hard-packed soil. *[Note: From research done on Sasquatch, or Big Foot sightings, it has been determined that it takes a weight of about one thousand pounds on a 14x7-inch foot to leave a one-inch-deep impression in hard soil.]* To their further shock, the officers then noticed that one of the giant tracks was actually superimposed *over* the tire track of the patrol car, clearly made *after* their first visit just minutes before! Police dogs were brought in, but the strange three-toed tracks vanished after 300 yards. An investigation was made and no evidence of a hoax could be found.

In the 1930s in New Jersey, the "Jersey Devil" was responsible for a long series of bizarre incidents in the Pine Barrens, a vast area of dense young pine trees. The Jersey Devil terrorized remote farmers and bootleggers for over a decade. The giant creature, never clearly seen, is even credited with chasing down and overturning a flatbed truck on a farm road one night.

There have been some creative hoaxes associated with these incidents, but a good percentage of the incidents were real. Those creatures had to come from—and go back to—somewhere. And often this creature activity coincides with nearby UFO sightings. A direct connection perhaps?

Twenty-five years ago in rural Arkansas, an event occurred similar to the South Carolina Scape Ore Swamp incident. In the Arkansas incident, however, bloodhounds chased the Big Foot-type creature into a thicket in a swamp and then surrounded the thicket. But not before a sheriff's posse had shot the ten-foot-tall creature to pieces with shotguns and high-powered rifles. According to the story, blood was everywhere. The mortally wounded Big Foot fell back into the thicket and the posse rushed in after it. Shock and disbelief overcame the posse when they found that the giant fur-covered creature had simply vanished.

These appearing and disappearing creatures probably use the same pathways, windows, corridors, portals, interdimensional phase shifts, or whatever, that the more highly evolved entities use. I put both groups in the same general category because of the similarity in the way they interact with humanity. It may one day be found that they are one and the same. But for now, I am going to keep the "lower" and "higher" categories separate.

After investigating a great many stories and incidents in the Sedona area, I have learned that in the vicinity of one particular spot, which measures roughly 200 by 300 yards, there have been individuals who have had the wits scared out of them by sighting some highly unusual creatures. No two sightings have been exactly the same.

In the spring of 1988 I invited Virgil (Posty) Armstrong to go to the area where my research had been centered. He agreed to come along. I felt fortunate, for I found Virgil to be one of the most exceptional clairvoyants I have ever met. We reached the spot and Virgil immediately began to psychically see and experience the same things I had been experiencing—and with no prompting from me.

We both sensed that there were two unseen entities nearby, and they were moving toward us from about a hundred yards out. One was to our left and one was directly in front. They were of a rather massive size and were not particularly hard to find. We were "watching" the entities and commenting on the impressions we were getting from them, when one veered off and started to go up into precipitous cliffs that were to our left. The being seemed to realize suddenly that it was being watched. It was soon undetectable to our perceptions.

The other one, however, remained where it was; it seemed to be curious. It also seemed to be a bit agitated about being openly observed. It didn't move and we didn't move, so to break the stalemate, we went toward it. It began to back away in a zigzag pattern, probably to see if it could throw us off. We continued to follow it, and the going got steep and rough. The entity went higher and higher in an effort to elude us. We came to an area of shelves that were like a series of stairs but were 10 to 15 feet high. We scrambled up the slope as far as we could go. We could sense that we were now very near to the unseen entity. It had reached the top of one of those ten-foot-high shelves and it seemed to know that we could not follow it.

We went to the base of one of the steplike shelves and we knew that the entity was just above us, not twenty feet away. We stood silently at the foot of the little cliff. I remarked, "Posty, are you feeling what I am?" He nodded in agreement as if he were about to say the same thing. As we walked closer to the base of the shelf, it felt as if a two-foot wide belt were tightening around our chests; the closer we got to the shelf, the tighter the sensation.

As we went still closer to the base of the shelf, the tightening continued, until there was discomfort in our chests and breathing became difficult. A half-dozen times we tested this effect. We walked away from the cliff, and after about 40 feet the sensation ceased. Going back toward the cliff again, the same chest tightening would return by degrees. It was no illusion. We discussed the matter and agreed that whatever it was, it was not trying to harm us. We knew that the physical sensation arose in close proximity to its energy field or aura. The entity finally moved upward into an area of caves and grottos, in the highest part of the canyon where we could not follow it.

A number of incidents have occurred in the Sedona area recently that reinforces the validity of what I have just described. An experienced local wilderness tour guide called me a few months ago and related the following incident. (Bear in mind that this man knew nothing about my research in the 200- by 300-yard spot. In particular, he knew nothing about the details of my close interaction with these beings.) He told me how he had led a group of hikers into a canyon that, unknown to him, was directly adjacent to my "spot." He was walking along when he had the sudden, distinct feeling that something was pacing him silently and unseen in the woods nearby.

This continued for fifteen minutes, when he realized that whatever "it" was, was now closing in on him. He said that as it came closer, it felt like his chest was in a vise. The closer it came, the tighter the viselike sensation in his chest. It got to the point where he had to stop walking. He explained to the group that he needed to rest for a bit. He sat down on a rock and described how a living, heavy energy field slowly and completely enveloped him. He said that he was not particularly frightened because whatever it was did not mean him any harm. He said somehow he knew that without any doubt. He said it felt like the entity was communicating, or attempting to communicate, with him. After about five minutes the sensations eased, and the entity disengaged and moved away into the forest. The guide got to his feet and continued the hike without discussing the incident with the group.

Three months ago I was introduced to a man who is an executive with a major Hollywood movie studio and very much into metaphysics. I had a long, detailed conversation with him and his attractive, young and inexperienced girlfriend about the supernatural, invisible beings I had found in the canyon. I could tell that his girlfriend thought I was nuts. I drew a detailed map and the next day they went to the spot.

Nothing really unusual happened until he and his girlfriend separated for awhile. (She needed to find a bush to retire behind.) She revealed to me later that on her way back to the trail she felt a presence, silent and unseen, coming slowly in her direction. It came into contact with her right side and slowly enveloped her. She said it felt like a heavy quietness—a stillness that had a warmth to it as it closed around her. At first she said she felt stark terror, but quickly was calmed from the soothing, unthreatening feeling she got from "it." The being departed minutes later and she was left with a feeling of total confusion. By the serious tone of her voice when she told me about what had happened, it was clearly evident she had had an experience that was very real to her.

Not long after meeting the aforementioned couple, I made the acquaintance of a German physician, Dr. Franz Beck. He is president of a large medical society in Germany, and is an exceptional clairvoyant as well as an avid hiker. Dr. Beck had discovered the spot on his own and had experienced the phenomena within it. And to my absolute, utter amazement, he had found the *exact* location and knew precisely where the boundaries of the spot began and ended!

These spots near Sedona are not the only ones, and they are certainly not unique to Sedona. My guess is that there are thousands of these spots in every region around the world. You may have one or more of these spots located near you.

*

A few weeks after I finished this chapter and before the manuscript was typeset, I met a local woman (Lila Lee Underwood, whose story is in Chapter 12) who has also had experiences with these entities. When she described how it felt when she interacted with these beings, I knew we were talking about the same thing. She then showed me five amazing photographs she had taken near the spot. She told me she was aware of its presence and asked it to allow its picture to be taken. Each of these photos has in it a blue, vaporous form that is not in the same position on any of the prints and is, in each case, a different size. I had a photo-lab technician look at the prints. He remarked that they were truly extraordinary photographs. I now have a full set of these amazing pictures in my collection of unusual photographs.

CHAPTER 8

Channeling Extraterrestrials

Channeling an extraterrestrial, no matter who they are, is an intriguing concept at the very least—and certainly controversial. It flies in the face of what we have been conditioned to believe. Organized religion has taught us that anything of this sort is surely the work of the devil.

I taught channeling to classes filled to capacity for two years. I was myself a public channel for a year and a half, channeling in open-forum sessions. I gained immeasurably from the experience. I would without hesitation recommend channeling to anyone who has an honest heart, grass-roots groundedness, a desire to help, and a firm belief in the connectedness of their own spirituality to Source. And most of all a strong belief in themselves as a human being.

Sedona's strongest virtue is for many the fact that it is a metaphysical refuge. A person can delve into the deepest questions concerning spiritual matters and not fear recrimination or reprisal from anyone—particularly relatives and/or religious groups. There is a very large, closeknit metaphysical family here, and it is a comforting, safe feeling. People have come here from everywhere to break away from bondage to imposed belief patterns elsewhere that were not palatable to them. They are the bold, new explorers in the New Age Frontier of self/spiritual unfoldment.

Channeling, in its different forms, is certainly an integral part of this new, free exploratory movement. Sedona has some of the best (clearest) channels in the world who either live here or have spent time here in the past. Not all of them channel verbally to an audience but rather channel information silently for themselves and others. Channeling, as was predicted by many at the start of its current boom in popularity, has leveled off and narrowed down to individuals who have had staying power.

It normally takes from one to two years of regular practice and effort to get "good" at channeling. I prefer the term "clear," because that really is what it amounts to. The clarity of a channel is that person's ability to maintain a particular focus. It's an ability to control the high-speed babble always present in our conscious and subconscious minds. This clarity allows messages of the entity being channeled to come through unaltered. Inner quiet within the channel permits an increasingly clearer connection to a spiritual or extraterrestrial personality.

I developed an inner quiet early in life and know its importance in connecting with "higher" entities. In a way, I had no choice but to develop an inner quiet. During the days of my childhood in rural Maine we were extremely poor, materially. We lived in a tiny house without running water and, for years, electricity. I was not raised by a television set because for a number of years we could not afford one. Somewhat like Thoreau, I spent a lot of time in the Maine woods alone. A great deal of time was spent in contemplation, sitting somewhere in a forest or field watching birds, clouds and flowers. I was meditating but didn't know it.

An accomplished channel at an advanced level of quieting the inner self faces certain complications. Only a few experienced channels know who they are really channeling. Sometimes they may believe it is a high spiritual Master but in reality the unseen personality may be a physical ET somewhere in near or far space. Presently there is an ongoing controversy about who is channeling whom. The resultant confusion and doubt has caused many first-rate channels to give it up altogether.

The problem is that it is not so much a diabolical deception on the part of an entity as it is an erroneous assumption or misconception on the part of the human channel. The problem, when it is present, is that everything "coming through" has to filter through the subconscious of the channel. If there are unmoving belief patterns within the mind of the channel, then the entity coming through cannot override or bypass those deeply entrenched beliefs. What you have then is a common situation whereby the choice of words or concepts are influenced by the channel's rigid beliefs, and as a result the telepathically transmitted messages are distorted. The messages then to a large extent reflect those beliefs and biases of the human channel. Thus the channel is actually channeling the desires of him/herself, not the pure undistorted messages of the being coming through. The subconscious in this case is editing material to suit its own tastes.

In channeling there are two different modes—full trance and conscious. In the full-trance state, the channel willingly goes into a deep half-sleep. This is an altered state of consciousness that leaves the person somewhat vulnerable to psychic attack or perhaps even possession. More on that later. The advantage here is that full-trance channels usually deliver messages more accurately, since the channel's personality is out of the way. It gives the channeled entity more room to maneuver. (That is, if the entity has the intelligence to say anything worthwhile.)

In the conscious mode of channeling, the channel is fully alert, fully conscious and in complete control of the situation, but has chosen to allow the unseen entity to use his or her physical and mental communication abilities to relay messages to a receptive audience. Maintaining clarity is difficult, because in this mode whatever is in the subconscious may often severely distort the message. That, as I said before, has long been a problem in channeling. That is why the genuinely crystal-clear channels are a national treasure.

Really clear men and women channels can bring us accurate spiritual or cosmic information that we can presently get in no other way. Yet after hearing information even from these great channels, our own intelligence, intuition and discernment must still be the final judge of the content of the message. There are those, unfortunately, who chart their lives by what has come through a particular channel. This is a trap. The term "giving your power away" has its most pointed application here. We have to steer our own boats. If we let someone else do it, we will eventually sink. It is important to consider the channeled information, weigh all factors, then decide.

There is an element in channeling overlooked, ignored, or unknown to many channels that can be dangerous to him or her. This lies in a channel's vulnerability to some entity's desire for control. Possession can be the result. In trance channeling particularly, unless the channel knows without a doubt who they are channeling, they can be putting themselves at enormous risk. In truth, there are intelligent, living entities unseen by us who, given the chance, will take total control of a human being—possession. But that only happens through the naive gullibility of the individual—or channel.

I have never personally seen a case of possession involving a *channel*. The fact is that *total* possession rarely happens. However, it can happen and it's not pretty. I have seen three authentic cases of it. In addition, any person who is in a state of extreme emotional instability or drug-induced lethargy is also vulnerable. One of the best ways to safeguard against any kind of ET or astral influence is to abstain from consciousness-altering substances and to solidly, completely and with total confidence align oneself with the highest white-light spiritual powers that be. Lord Michael—or to some, Archangel Michael—is an energy, a visualization I would always recommend if you are in search of a higher teacher. There are many, however. There is a tremendous power of protection from the "Ascended Master" level of spirituality. One might ask, "How do you know that Lord Michael is a spiritual being and not an extraterrestrial?" I would say that maybe he is, in actuality, an "extraterrestrial"—as may be Jesus as well. The "highest," most advanced beings, both spiritual and extraterrestrial, may well operate from both levels. As one fellow put it, "They may all park their ships in the same garage."

The guidelines I have given are ones that I and others have used with great success. I have consciously channeled ten completely different entities, and I have never been harmed in any way. And I have complete faith that I never will. Wherever the Creator energy or light is, there should never be any reason for fear. No being not of the "light" will ever challenge that Creator energy.

I channeled off and on a nonhuman ET named Kaal for nearly a year. I knew who he was, and there was not the slightest deception on his (its) part. Channeling a being with the type of energy he has is very difficult and draining (for me), but I felt, and still feel, that it was a wonderful opportunity and experience. I regularly channeled up to six beings at different times and learned to recognize who they were by the feel of their energy as they approached. Djwhal Khul (see the Alice Bailey books) is light, loving and easy to channel, as is Vywamus, although Vywamus is a bit more intense. Sanat Kumara, whom I usually channel, is an almost overwhelming energy at times. But Kaal was five times as intense. I could rarely channel Kaal for more than an hour before my own energy would rapidly begin to wane.

Be wary of some of the messages coming through some channels. If it sounds like the messages are coming from a confused ten-year-old with ego problems, they probably are. In my opinion, the greatest channeled entity ever may be the entity Seth, who came through Jane Roberts in Elmira, New York, beginning in the late sixties. The Seth books probably contain some of the most accurate information ever to come through a channel. Edgar Cayce was another great channel.

No doubt one of the better ET channels in the world is Robert Shapiro of Sedona. Bob has been channeling professionally for eleven years two ETs—one named Zoosh (pronounced Zoesh) and one named Joopah (pronounced Hoopah). I've heard him channel on many occasions. With many channels, depending on his or her own channel-sustaining energy level, the information coming through can be either boringly mundane or awesomely inspiring. When Bob is tuned in perfectly, he is unmatched by anyone—a respectable and well-earned position for a channel.

In closing this chapter I need to add that *all* paranormal activity in any form is somehow interrelated—be it UFOs, ETs, channeling, psychic activity, manifestation, spiritual activity, vortexes, etc.

So it is all part and parcel of one whole picture. I think at times we tend to be somewhat linear, and focus on one or two narrow areas, which can be, I think, severely to our detriment.

CHAPTER 9

More Extraterrestrial Encounters

I would venture a guess that if someone were to go to a place such as Syracuse, Little Rock, San Antonio, Key West, Pocatello, Des Moines or Spokane and dig around for two years as I did here, that person would come up with as much material as I have about Sedona.

The following incidents and encounters are a broad representation of UFO/ET encounters by area residents and visitors. My opinion is that many of these incidents resulted in the abduction of the individuals involved. I have talked at length with most of these people. It's difficult to put into words the sincerity and concern that was reflected in their voices and faces about what they had experienced. When a mature man or woman breaks down emotionally over a UFO experience they are reliving in an interview, this is to me strong evidence that the person is not lying or simply making up a story. I feel fortunate to have shared in their experiences, and I share in turn these experiences here with you. Several of the people written about in this chapter volunteered to be hypnotized. To them I express my thanks.

Previously these people had nowhere to turn to explain their predicament. Who would ever believe them? Now, however, there are a growing number of support groups worldwide for these people. They can now openly discuss what happened to them and vent some of the feelings connected to the experience.

Due to the fact that abduction scenarios are now so well documented in best-selling books such as *Intruders*, *Missing Time*, *The Andreasson Affair*, and *Communion*, I have opted not to devote lengthy explorations using hypnosis on abductions in this book. Human abductions by aliens always seem to adhere to the following general patterns. A UFO, or particularly an odd skyborne light, is sighted. After intently watching the UFO or light or some other similar phenomenon, the individual then discovers that a period of time is missing, usually one to two hours (providing, that is, there is any memory at all).

In some cases the individual is left with symmetrical or geometrical scars. Sometimes there is a vague recollection of an instrument being inserted into the body. Usually, at this time (if it is remembered) the abductee tries to ignore or blot out the unpleasant, dreamlike memory, until at some point—usually years later—the rest of the picture begins to unfold. Under hypnosis (if it is a genuine abduction) these people tell of being transported to a ship, often by *extremely* nonhuman-looking creatures; of being disrobed, examined—sometimes painfully—and then returned to the point of the abduction or nearby. Human-type ETs *seem* to be doing little or no abductions and implantations. There have been credible reports of human aliens watching abductee examinations being performed by nonhuman aliens. Why?

Could it be that there is some kind of a military-type command structure or hierarchy, and that one or all groups or races come under the directorship of another? Are the aliens encountered most often the workers, the rank and file, the soldiers? And if so, who are the "higher-ups" and what is their ultimate role in all of this? It seems that a percentage of abductions are being performed by genuinely compassionate and caring aliens. The abductees in these cases were often left with a feeling of almost euphoric bliss after their return. Some of these human participants were shown things so marvelous during their abduction that they longed for a return of the alien visitors.

JOHN LARSON

This account of an event that occurred several years ago was related to me by a local man. It involved his uncle, and the location was the Yuba River wilderness in northern California. The incident is unique in UFO lore.

In the fall of 1985 John Larson's uncle, who is a prominent California political figure, was bow hunting in the Sierra Nevada Mountains near the Yuba River. He had gone out hunting alone early in the morning and was carefully stalking along a well-traveled deer trail. He was walking almost noiselessly. He rounded a bend in the trail and was stunned by an unexpected sight ahead of him. There, not twenty yards away, stood six four-feet-tall humanlike creatures. The creatures were dressed military fashion in silvery blue metallic uniforms. The creatures were not immediately aware of his intense scrutiny. A moment later, they were alerted to his presence and turned quickly to face him.

Their countenances revealed that they were as surprised as he was. The California man could see that the little creatures resembled human children in proportion but they had grayish skin and shockingly large eyes. John's uncle, experiencing extreme fright and near panic, raised his bow to show that he was armed and ready to defend himself. As the man brought up his bow, one of the small humanoids reached down and pulled something from his belt and pointed it toward him. The hunter said all he remembered was being hit head to foot by something that felt like gas. Then he blacked out.

When he came to he was lying face down on the ground at the edge of the trail. He peered at his watch and saw that it was almost four o'clock. He had been unconscious over five hours. He got up, brushed the sand and pine needles off and began to take inventory of his condition. He decided he was in good shape and seemed to be unharmed. Then he got another shock. He looked over at his aluminum-alloy bow and quiver of aluminum arrows. He saw that they had been melted, had cooled, and now lay in long, hardened silvery pools on the ground.

ROBERT WEAVER

Robert, now 36, grew up in a straitlaced cattle town in central Texas. No one had ever heard of a UFO or a space alien in his town. If they had, the last thing they would do would be to talk about it. Robert has had a series of baffling events that began at the age of ten. Always after each episode he was left deeply perplexed and confused.

It all started one winter day twenty-six years ago. He had finished doing his chores in the family's sprawling cattle barn. He had picked up some tools and was on his way back to the ranch house, happy to be done for the day. About halfway to the house, he abruptly realized that he was becoming immobilized by something. He also knew that whatever it was, it was directly overhead in the sky. He distantly heard the metal tools clatter to the ground as he released his grip on them.

The next thing he knew, he was in the ranch house sitting at the big kitchen table. It was now dark out and it was very late. His dad was quite angry with him, informing him that he had been gone more than half the night. He demanded to know where Robert had been, but Robert could offer no explanation. What made matters worse, after several more of these occurrences, the locals began to cast sidelong glances at him, as if there were something wrong with him.

Robert was treated coolly during his growing years by some of the townspeople and some of his relatives. They were convinced that he was a rather strange boy. Something was "wrong" with him, although they could never really put their finger on it. This unexplainable activity continued at irregular intervals in his life.

In 1989 he decided he had finally had enough. He was ready to do something about it. His decision was made one night when he awoke at 2:00 a.m. and found that a blindingly bright blue light was beaming onto his chest through the open bedroom window. His wife was sleeping soundly beside him. He could make no effort to wake her, as he could barely move his head. He managed to look out the open window. High above the roof of his neighbor's house he could make out the shape of a large, cigar-shaped object outlined around the blue light.

The alien abductors may have made a mistake, for this time he was able to remember being floated out of the house *through the open window* and into the cigar-shaped craft. He said he was then examined by five-foot-tall creatures that more resembled insects than humans. The creature who was checking him over told Robert telepathically to try and relax because no harm would come to him. At that point his memory of the rest of his stay on the ship fails.

Robert is one of a growing number of abductees who are determined to find out what has been happening to them and why. He confided to me that after one episode of missing time, he returned with unexplainable scars on his lower back for which no logical explanation could be found, after lengthy and expensive medical tests were made. He had lower back pain for months after the event.

GORDON TODD

At the beginning of the book I mentioned a network, or grapevine, in Sedona that loosely formed when word went around that I was writing a book on UFO encounters. I am sure that I never would have known of such incidents as the following one had it not been for that informal network. I know that uncountable people have had Gordon's type of experience but they either shrug it off or rationalize it into something normal and explainable.

Gordon phoned me one evening. As I talked with him, I noted the concern in his voice. He related to me that while watching television in his recliner chair the night before, he had dozed off and awakened in the predawn hours. Upon awakening, he was immediately aware that something dry and crusty filled his mustache. It also coated his chin and the front of his shirt. When he saw that it was indeed blood, he became quite alarmed. He went to the mirror and found its source. On the tip of his nose was a tiny puncture wound. There was not a drop of blood inside his nose or any other marks on his face or mouth from which the blood could have come. He said it was hard to believe that so much blood could have come from such a small puncture.

I inquired about insects and he quickly replied that there was no discoloration or swelling whatsoever around the tiny red wound that would indicate the bite of a spider, bee, scorpion, etc. If that were all there was to the story, it could quite easily be attributed to something common and explainable—like an unusual nosebleed or ruptured vein. But often it is peripheral, or seemingly unrelated factors that make a seemingly insignificant event *very* significant. For instance, several days prior to the bloody-shirt incident Gordon had been hearing deep, vibrating/humming noises in various parts of his house. This had been going on periodically for several weeks, but had not been particularly alarming or bothersome. He mentioned to me that he had also been aware of this same vibrating/humming sound *inside* the room just before he dozed off that night. The sound had been growing in volume, but instead of going to investigate as he normally would, strangely—he fell asleep.

Gordon was informed enough to realize that it may have been ETs in his room that night. In his daily meditation he made it absolutely clear that his personal space had been violated. He claimed that it was his universal right *not* to have something unknown imposed on him by aliens against his free will. He reinforced his affirmation of protection with white light. The house noises and bodily intrusions have not returned.

Gordon's experience wasn't the only one. There were six similar incidents that I investigated in Sedona in that same four-month span. During this time there were some highly unusual sounds and activity in the living quarters of a number of local residents. My apartment was one of them.

The same month that I started my UFO investigation there were some frighteningly eerie beeps, dronings, buzzing and snapping sounds in our apartment that usually began after we were sound asleep. We dealt with this in much the same way Gordon did. The final straw for me was on one quiet, windless night. We awoke abruptly, and we heard in the dark room a sound somewhat like that of small sheets flapping and snapping rapidly in a strong wind, or like the flapping of wings. Two other residents of our apartment building also heard these same sounds in their rooms at night. If this has ever happened to you, you know exactly what I am talking about.

SUSAN BEDELL

Another Sedona resident, Susan Bedell, had an interesting story about her niece, who visited her from the East. The girl, in her early twenties, had come to stay for a week. The house was small, so the girl slept on the large sofa in the living room. One night in the early morning hours the girl was startled awake by the sound of someone moving around in the kitchen. She explained later that it sounded like two or three people carefully rummaging through drawers and pots and pans looking for something. The rustling and clinking noises were accompanied by bright lights that were moving slowly about in the kitchen.

From where she lay, the girl could only see into the left corner of the kitchen and the activity was at the other end. Nervously, she called out her aunt Susan's name and got no reply. Worse yet, the kitchen noises ceased abruptly. Then the girl became extremely frightened. She thought someone had broken into the house, and that everyone else was asleep. The girl never gave a thought to any possibility but burglars.

Then about six feet from the girl a dim light appeared several feet off the floor. The light grew steadily until it was a glowing column five feet high. It gradually took on the form of a person until a minute later a four-feet-tall humanoid creature stood staring at her, statuelike. Although the girl had never heard of Whitley Strieber or his books *Communion* or *Transformation*, Susan later said that her niece's description of the being that appeared in front of her was identical to the ones in Strieber's books—disproportionately large head, gray skin, large, slanted almond eyes and a body that seemed too frail to hold itself up. The girl got a good look at it.

The girl stared at the being, and it stared back for several minutes. Then slowly it vanished in the same manner it had appeared. The kitchen and the living room were once again in darkness. This was the only incident that the niece had of that type—that she can remember.

BONNIE HAYNES

Bonnie moved to Sedona several years ago from Taos, New Mexico. While in Taos, she had had some highly paranormal experiences, one of which was of a recurring "dream" of beings who took her seven-year-old daughter away for an examination. They told her that her daughter would not be harmed and would be returned to her. Bonnie would have no part of it, and objected loudly and emotionally. She screamed at them, and pleaded for someone to help her.

Suddenly there was a flash of dazzling white light, and an angelic-looking woman dressed in white materialized. The apparition looked at Bonnie and then turned to the beings taking the daughter. She ordered them to give the child back. The little men complied, and Bonnie took the little girl and fled. A dream? At that time Bonnie had no knowledge of UFOs or alien abductions.

In a separate dream she has had terrifying visions of being forcibly taken from her bed by what she terms "horrible-looking humanoid creatures." These beings take her, hold her down and insert something into her mid-spinal area. In the dream she realizes what is going on, so she fights. She kicks violently to try to defend herself but the creatures continue in a cold, mechanical manner as if they simply have a job to do and they are going to finish it. They seemed to have no regard whatsoever for her emotional well-being. Bonnie had debilitating pain in her middle back for a week after the "dream" and had to seek medical attention.

The similarity between Bonnie's "dreams" and documented UFO abduction cases is disturbing. I interject here a similar experience of a North Carolina woman who now works and lives in Sedona. She also had a dream that was so vivid and real, she refuses to acknowledge it as simply a dream.

She tells of humanoid creatures coming into her bedroom one night when she lived in South Carolina (at a time of several local UFO sightings). While she lay on her stomach totally immobile, one of the beings showed her a syringelike instrument with a long, gold needle on the end. He told her that they "have to" insert this into the back of her head and will try to make it as painless as possible. They insert the needle into her brain, causing near-unbearable pain. The next day she, like Bonnie, had pain so severe that she had to seek medical attention.

In Taos Bonnie was on her way one day to preschool to pick up one of her children. Out of nowhere flew an unusually large, very "beautiful" golden eagle. It flew over her car and seemed almost to be beckoning her to follow. She didn't follow it then, but several days later she felt drawn to go where the eagle had gone. She traveled in the direction she had seen the eagle fly, taking a seldom-used ranch road. She drove to a flat, grassy area of Taos where there were no houses nearby. She came to a barren, open area ringed by a half-dozen tall trees.

She saw at once, to her and her son's delight, that there were three of these "beautiful eagles" waiting for them in the trees. She said that after that day and over a period of months she had been called to that area over a dozen times by the eagles. In one instance she was at the house of a friend when the eagles called. As a result, she brought along her friend and her friend's two children to see the eagles too. The eagles were indeed waiting and were plainly seen by the two adults and two children. She interpreted the eagle experience as one of a mystical nature, with both Indian and spiritual overtones. Taos is strongly imbued with both philosophies.

I would venture to say that this was a case of "screen memory." Often when there is alien contact, the contactees are left not with a memory of seeing and/or interacting with terrifying-looking humanoid aliens but with alluring, large, soft-eyed, friendly deer, owls, eagles or some other nonthreatening animal or bird. This kind of overlaid image may also be associated with the abductee's subconscious, which refuses to accept what it has experienced and replaces it with something more comfortable. Or more likely this image was transmitted to the abductee by the aliens themselves to conceal the real event. So when something triggers a memory of aliens, the mind reverts to the false, misleading memory of a Bambi-like deer standing near a fuzzy silvery object—which, under deep hypnosis, turns out to be a flying saucer.

For anyone these days, especially in any type of a UFO incident, to be fanciful, gullible and unaware is an unfavorable position, due to the current magnitude of the activities of alien beings. A fair percentage of our population falls into that category.

KATHY MILLER

This incident occurred in June 1967 when Kathy was sixteen years old and living in the seaside community of Santa Barbara, California. She had had a heated argument with her parents and had left the house to walk on the beach. It was about 8:30 p.m. On the way she met her friend Jerry, who went along with her. They started for an undeveloped area called Moore Mesa, which is a rolling plateau above the beach a relatively short distance from her house.

They walked along the mesa enjoying each other's company as sixteen-year-olds will. They talked about some of the silly things they had been doing lately for fun—such as snake-hunting from the hood of a car. This entailed driving around the sandy coastal areas of Santa Barbara, with one person sitting on the hood of the car. Someone would yell "Snake!" and the driver would slam on the brakes. The hood-sitter would then go sliding off to chase the snake. They shared giggles over this as they strolled along. By now night had fallen but visibility on the trail was good, as the moon was full. Suddenly they both realized at the same time that some-one was following them. They spun around, and less than twenty feet behind them on the darkened trail were seven beings that they thought at first were penguins.

Moments later upon closer inspection, they saw that they weren't gazing at penguins at all but some sort of three-feet tall creatures with large, round eyes. The creatures had on garments resembling black jumpsuits with a bold white V pattern down to the waistline. Kathy and Jerry began to run as fast as they could toward the beach. It was the only direction they could go to get back to town. They ran hundreds of yards before they turned, and to their horror saw that the little creatures were still behind them, at the same distance they had been before. The creatures were not even breathing hard. It was as if they hadn't been running at all.

The teenagers ran on down to the beach, turned again, and watched as the seven small beings filed into a cluster of low bushes. After a while, curiosity overcame their fright. The two teens decided to go up to the bushes to see if the strange little men would talk to them. They walked to the patch of bushes and called to the creatures, but there was no reply. They called again and again but still there was no answer from the bushes. The teens talked it over for a minute and decided they had better get home while the getting was still good.

When the two teenagers arrived home, they were met by furious parents. It was almost 12:30 a.m. The youngsters discovered that over three hours of time were missing...they thought it was 9:30!

TIM CLARK

Tim is an Oregon resident and tells of this 1970 incident while driving through the Mojave Desert in California. Strong emotion is reflected in his voice as he relives this encounter. From my point of view, that is a good indication the event happened just as the individual experienced it.

He describes how he was driving through the desert just before dawn. A blazing sphere of orange light passed over his car and landed in a broad, sandy plain nearby. Tim noted that for some reason he was not at all fearful of this sudden strange appearance. It had a familiarity about it somehow. He pulled over to the shoulder of the highway to get a better look at the object. Without knowing exactly why, he found himself with an overpowering urge to get out of his car and walk over to the landed object. The radiance from the sphere was so bright he had no trouble walking to within fifty yards of it. He knew this was as far as he could safely go.

As he stood there, the near-blinding orange light began to subside. Soon the detailed features of a solid, physical ship came into full view. Even though the ship's light was low, the surrounding area glowed surrealistically with an orange luminosity. A doorway opened at the base of the craft and a human male appeared in the opening. He was about 6'5" tall and appeared to be in his late thirties. The athletic-looking man moved toward Tim with the agility of a jungle cat and then stood motionless before him. The tall man said nothing, but instead put both his hands on Tim's shoulders, looked into his eyes for a few moments and then...went back to the ship.

In minutes the ship was again surrounded by a fiery orange light. It lifted off silently, flying to the north at a terrific speed, and was soon out of sight. Tim says that he has no idea why the encounter occurred. He mentioned that he had a "suntan" on his face for a few days afterward.

I have read of many UFO encounters and have talked to a number of people who have had close experiences with orange lights. Although Tim's story is by far the most explicit and perhaps the most dramatic, it seems that the ships of the "good guys" are almost always enshrouded with this bright orange light. The contacts with these orange lights and the beings associated with them always seem to be of a distinctly positive nature.

SPACE BROTHERS?

Most UFO researchers very much disfavor the term "space brothers" and "space sisters." Those human-looking beings, as in Tim Clark's story, may be as close as we are going to get. The space-brother movement has, right from its beginning in the 1940s, been fraught with illogical connotations and a Flash Gordon kind of illusionary/mystical, wishful thinking. A modern fairy tale. We cannot afford any more to be gullible or blindly accepting at this point—we just cannot. Utmost discernment *must* now be our guide to keep us from falling into another space-brother cult type of mentality. It was thought for years that all of them out there were our space brothers and sisters. Even now a segment of the New Age movement still religiously hangs on to this kind of thinking. We now have substantial evidence that indicates there are at least two races or species of aliens who are anything *but* our brothers and sisters from space!

This next incident is an example of what I would attribute to the malevolent space visitors. There is a retired couple, whom I will call Laura and Steven, who live in Sedona and who had a less-than-pleasant meeting with ufonauts. I relate the story as it was indirectly told to me.

According to the account, the couple were watching television one evening when they noticed a flaring blue-white light falling to earth near their property. They interpreted this as a crash landing of an airplane. They rushed from their house and, after a short scramble through the red rock desert, found the crash site. They expected to see smoldering wreckage and passengers in dire need. Instead they came upon a disc-shaped craft, and around it were small men with large heads busily gathering samples of the surrounding terrain.

The woman uttered some sort of cry, a sound that attracted the attention of the little men. Realizing they had been seen, the couple turned and ran as fast as their legs would carry them. As they struggled over the crest of a low hill, they were hit in the back and knocked down by something that caused searing pain. The pair then lost consciousness. When the couple came to, it was midday and they were now three miles from where they had been the night before. To their further consternation, they discovered they had fresh scars and marks on their bodies, marks not attributable to flight through cactus and bush!

MARTIN GROFF

The following incident was related to me by a Prescott, Arizona, man. Prescott is forty miles south of Sedona on Highway 89A. This is one of the lighter, more pleasantly inspiring stories concerning ETs that I have come across. Martin had a meeting of some sort at his house, and among the ten or twelve people present was a very striking young couple. As the evening wore on, Martin found himself sitting next to a man who was the only smoker in the room. The smoker grew uneasy because the ash on his cigarette lengthened to an inch and there was not an ashtray in sight. Everyone in the room noticed his predicament as he held the cigarette over his open palm.

Some of the guests began looking around the room for a proper receptacle when suddenly from a far corner of the room, a heavy glass ashtray rose into the air. The ashtray drifted smoothly across the room toward the smoker. By now everyone in the room was aghast at the unexpected sight of the levitating ashtray—all except the young couple. Martin saw that they regarded the whole thing with barely concealed amusement. The heavy ashtray continued gliding across the room at knee height and settled just beneath the cigarette of the incredulous smoker. With a quick tap of the edge of the ashtray on the extended cigarette, the ash fell neatly into it. The ashtray then settled softly on a small table at the center of the room. While the rest of the guests were excitedly carrying on about the amazing spectacle, Martin kept an eye on the young couple who were keeping a low profile.

It had been a late evening, and as the guests began to leave Martin still closely but unobtrusively observed the attractive young couple. Martin is a long-time UFO buff and his suspicions about the couple grew minute by minute. Called away for a moment into another room, he was distracted from his chance to engage the couple in conversation. When he finally did break away, he was told that they had left just moments before. Martin hurried out of the house in the direction they had gone, but they were nowhere to be seen.

On a hunch he rushed back into the house to get a flashlight. Earlier that day Martin had done some landscaping in the front yard, so most of the area was still freshly raked, smooth and wet. As he had thought, the couple had left perfect tracks in the loose, wet soil. He would follow and perhaps overtake them before they got to their car. He followed the tracks for a short distance to the corner of his property. There the tracks abruptly ended. Martin made wide circles around the last set of tracks—there were no others. The mysterious young couple had vanished...vanished into thin air!

Years ago while living in Santa Cruz County, California, I had an experience somewhat similar to Martin's. (When I moved from Santa Cruz to Sedona in 1987, I had a driving, almost fanatical urge not only to get to Sedona but to get out of Santa Cruz as fast as possible. It turned out that the epicenter of the devastating 1989 Bay Area earthquake was only a few miles from the house I was living in.)

The experience I had was rather novel and I am convinced that they were aliens. In the early '80s when I first moved to Santa Cruz, I had been reading all sorts of UFO, alien, occult, channeled, space brother/sister and psychic stuff and listened to every channel within fifty miles. Finally, by degrees I began to focus on the alien phenomena which, from a rational, logical viewpoint, got me nowhere. One day, feeling totally exasperated and fed up with all if it, I looked to the sky and shouted, "All right! I'll make a deal! If you spacemen really exist, meet me at Star of the Sea Park on Monday afternoon at one o'clock—sharp!" I was serious!

The anticipated Monday came around and I left work at 12:30 to take my lunch hour at the park. The park at that time of year was always deserted during the week. I sat in my car eating my lunch and listening to the radio, carefully scanning the area for anything suspicious. It was a chilly day of alternating sun and fog. I had my windows rolled up against the chill, and being a novice about UFOs, I fully expected that if anything did show up, it would be green, very alien and sport multiple octopuslike appendages. I was confident it would look like something out of a sci-fi novel and would be named Zorg, Zork, Klug or something similar. It would come bounding out of nowhere, tap on my window and introduce itself. It got close to one o'clock.

The parking lot could easily hold a hundred cars and mine was the only one there. Nothing was happening. Then at exactly one o'clock—and I mean exactly one o'clock to the second—an old, battered, tan-colored Chevy pickup with a camper shell on the back pulled into the space beside me. "Damn!" I remember thinking. "Now the aliens won't come for sure!" An average-looking woman about twenty-five years old with sandy blonde hair stepped out of the pickup. She was carrying a baby in her arms that appeared to be about a year and a half old. She spread a blanket carefully in front of the pickup truck and began reading a magazine and eating a light lunch. I was still waiting but it didn't look like the aliens were going to show up.

I sat looking at the lightly dressed young mother and her baby. It was a cold day—forty-five to fifty degrees. She had placed the blanket in the shade of a large pine tree, although there was a nice, sunny sheltered area about a hundred feet farther. The baby was nearly naked and they both sat contentedly, she reading a book and munching vegetables and the baby playing quietly with a small toy. I thought the whole thing was a bit odd, but didn't attach any real significance to it, until I started to leave to go back to work.

As I backed up and then drove slowly past the mother and the baby, the baby caught my attention with a piercing stare. While holding my attention with that riveting expression, the child raised its arm and gave me a coordinated, adultlike farewell wave that was not at all typical of an eighteen-month-old infant. It took me about a week to connect the incident to aliens and I kicked myself resoundingly for perhaps missing the chance of a lifetime. They had indeed showed up!

BILL LEWIS

Bill Lewis was a long-time Sedona resident, but in spite of my best efforts, I have been unable to locate him. I believe he no longer lives in Sedona, so I am going to relate this incident as a synopsis of a story that appeared in the October 1988 issue of *Windwords* magazine.

Bill had been attending a series of seminars in awareness training in Phoenix. He was driving home to Payson from the first seminar in the early morning hours. He was part way home when the headlights, domelights and dash gauges in his car began going on and off in an alternating sequence. The engine stalled and restarted several times. This was over a time span of about 15 seconds. He made it home but did not want to trust his car for the return trip to the next day's seminar. For the return drive he borrowed his father's new Cadillac convertible.

In his words: "I was in an incredibly joyful state of mind when I left the seminar Sunday evening. I was going to drive out to the edge of town (Phoenix) and flip the top down, but I couldn't stop the car! It was like it was on rails. I became more and more frustrated because I couldn't stop the car even though I wanted to. This went on for about 50 miles." *[Note: I know of four other incidents very similar to this one and they all occurred within miles of one another.]*

"It was like I was compelled to drive, and I was driving faster than I normally would—about 80 mph or so. I couldn't bring myself to stop the car." Approximately 50 miles north of Phoenix on Highway 87, he heard a voice commanding him to stop the car. He pulled far off the highway, got out and found himself walking away from the car, up into a small, desolate side valley. "All of a sudden I got this incredible sense of dread. I felt threatened. The hair stood up on the back of my neck and I felt a chill go up my spine. I was terrified. I saw a light over my shoulder and, although I couldn't remember turning, I found myself turned around, facing down this little valley. Part of me was terrified and part of me was exhilarated. I was paralyzed; I couldn't move.

"The whole little valley was just bright light. It was almost like tangible light, like the light had substance. The whole valley was lit up with this incredibly brilliant white light." Next, without knowing how he got there, he found himself back in his father's

Cadillac driving home to his wife and kids. When he arrived, they told him the trip had taken him three hours and fifteen minutes, over an hour longer than normal.

The next case involves the father of a Sedona woman. The incident occurred near Cave Creek, Arizona, which, like several others, took place in the same general area as the Bill Lewis/Cadillac incident—an area of repeated UFO/paranormal contacts.

I'll call this man Gary. Gary was driving through the desert when the engine of his car began to cut out, then stalled entirely. He pulled off the road and got out to determine what the problem was. He had the hood up and was looking at the engine when a blonde man walked out of the barren desert toward him. The man told Gary that he was not from this planet and said he would return in four months and take Gary up in his ship. The stranger then turned and disappeared back into the desert. Gary's car started normally after the stranger's departure. The mysterious man left Gary with an impression of great kindness, gentleness and wisdom.

Gary was then of advanced years and was in extremely poor health. At that point the wild notion of taking a ride in space in a flying saucer sounded just fine to him. The kind stranger did, indeed, come back for Gary in four months and took him for a ride in his ship. The elderly gentleman told of his wonderful experience to a handful of trusted friends. The old man died shortly after.

＊

The following incidents are more that were included at the eleventh hour—just before publication. (UFO accounts are still coming in daily through the network.)

Regarding this incident, I must again be cautiously vague about identities. In this particular case I am exceptionally cautious and less detailed because of the positions of the individuals involved. One of them is one of this country's top politicians. Often by necessity I insulate myself as much as I can from possible interferences so that I can carry on this research. The credibility of the participants in this UFO encounter are 100% reliable.

In 1986 a pilot with a major U.S. airline was driving south from Sedona to Prescott, Arizona, on Highway 89A. Passing the summit of Mingus Mountain, he noticed bright flashes of light coming from a side canyon. He left his car to investigate the area, and in the side canyon he saw a landed disc-shaped craft sitting on the ground and three humanoid beings walking around it. The three humanoids were aware of him immediately. One of them raised an arm high in a gesture of greeting. The pilot became rather unhinged at that point and made a dash for his car.

Once back on the highway, he accelerated his car to a high speed in order to distance himself as much as possible from the disc. The disc rapidly caught up with him and passed over the car, positioning itself in front of him—seemingly in an effort to slow him down or stop him. Shortly after, the disc flew away.

Twenty miles later he reached Prescott, and upon arrival called a politician friend. The friend asked if he wanted to tell his story to the Air Force. The pilot agreed, and within hours he was contacted by Air Force personnel and was on his way to Wright-Patterson Air Force Base in Ohio in an Air Force jet. After landing, he was quickly ushered into a hangar somewhere on the base. (Could it have been Hangar 18?)

He waited patiently in a room for thirty minutes and then, to his surprise, he was told that no questions would be asked of him. He was then returned to Prescott in another Air Force jet.

This incident took place in the same general area as the Bill Lewis/Cadillac incident. There have now been so many reports of this type from the Payson-Black Canyon-Prescott area that serious research and investigation there is warranted.

CHAPTER 10

Erika Porter

The case of Erika Porter, a long-time Sedona resident, is so involved and compelling that her story has enough information for an entire book. Perhaps in the future I will be in a position to write it. However, for now I will recount portions of her story here. The following is in her own words.

"We were driving down the road one day. It was a narrow two-lane road, and we passed an old man bent over a dog that had just been hit. Traffic was really heavy that day because it was Christmas. The road was real narrow, and I had a hard time finding a place to turn around to go back. I finally found a place to turn. I came back and had to turn around again to get in back of this guy's parked camper.

"As we come upon him, he is *still* bent over the dog in the same position. By now ten minutes have gone by—and he hasn't moved! So we go up to talk to him. He's an older guy with a really dumpy-looking camper. He's fifty-fiveish, slim, grey hair—and the most startling, striking blue eyes you have ever seen in your life. If he had looked at me with those eyes and said, 'Get in the camper—we are going somewhere,' I think I would have gone *anywhere* with this guy!

"Anyway, my friend and I are bent down to do Reiki on the dog. The man says, 'What are you doing?' We reply, 'Well...we are just going to do some Reiki on the dog.' He didn't say, 'What the hell's that?' Then we asked him, 'Did you see the dog get hit?' He said, 'No. I *heard* the dog hit.' I remember thinking, 'Well, that's weird.' So the guy says to us, 'I think we should take the dog to the vet.' And I said, 'On Christmas? We would never find one open!' Anyhow, the guy says he knows where there is one. Then he says, 'Let's load the dog in your van.' Now, this guy could have taken the dog in his own camper and gone with him. You know what I mean.

"We end up going to the vet. We get to the vet's house first, and this guy that looks like a Hell's Angel comes to the door and asks me what I want. He tells us he is watching the place for the vet who is off for Christmas. We tell him that we have this dog in our van that got hit, that's not ours. And we have this other *unknown* guy who's coming behind us that we've never seen before. I stood there thinking how stupid that sounded.

"So this guy at the door, that's got tattoos all over him, looks at me and growls, 'This is Christmas! You ain't going to get the vet up here *tonight!*'" (She snaps her fingers.) "Two seconds later, the vet pulls up! The guy in the camper pulls up! It was just like the whole thing was orchestrated.

"So the vet goes to the van, examines the dog, then comes over to us and says, 'I'm sorry; there really is nothing I can do.' Then he walked back over to the others and started talking to them. These guys were all dressed in blue jackets—which we thought was strange.

"While we were waiting, I talked to the guy with the blue eyes. I asked him if he lived around here. He replied that no, he wasn't from here and then he says, 'And Alice is back at the house.' Alice is my mother and earlier I had been wondering if she would get here for Christmas. I didn't have much time to think about that one, because the vet came over and said they would have to put the dog to sleep. We replied, 'Well, we only want the best for the dog...so okay, if that's what you have to do.'

"We walked outside and this Hell's Angel biker guy walks us to our van. Now, I mean this guy is the scroungiest looking cowboy you have ever seen. He turns to us and says—deliberately, calmly, in a totally different tone of voice, 'Perhaps our paths will cross again.' And as he walked away, I remember thinking, 'What? Wait a minute!'

"So we get back in the van and begin driving to Phoenix. About halfway there we realize that two hours of time are missing."

This next incident, which Erika also related to me, took place in northern California several years ago. Again, in her own words.

"A friend and I had gone to Salem, Oregon, to visit her granddaughter. Then we were returning down through California and going over to Reno. I was driving. Leda and I had gotten to the town of Dunsmuir just after midnight to get gas. Dunsmuir is near Mt. Shasta. I think it was around twelve-ten, twelve-fifteen in the morning, somewhere in that area. We had gone through Dunsmuir and everything was closed. We had started across on the road to Susanville on Route 89, which goes through the Shasta and Lassen National Forests. I hadn't been on that road for about fourteen years. I thought that by now there would be a gas station on it. We were driving her car. It was a small one and we had about a half tank of gas. This was only about six gallons of gas—not much if you have to go 135 miles over mountainous terrain, but we thought a gas station would be open halfway there.

"There was very little traffic on the road that night. And that night there were animals galore, moving around and crossing the highway. There were deer, elk and small animals, so I slowed down to about forty-five miles an hour to avoid hitting them. We were about thirty minutes out of Dunsmuir up in the mountains when I noticed that a light just appeared behind me. Well, I thought, that was strange because I hadn't seen any side roads where a car might have come from. So I thought one was just gaining on us because we were going so slow. But the car didn't come any faster. It didn't gain on me at all.

"Well, I just drove that way for several minutes. I didn't want to alarm Leda. I must have driven about fifteen minutes that way and the light just stayed behind me. So finally I woke her up and I said, 'I don't know what we've got back there, but I just have a feeling it's something that's not normal.' Leda is kind of feisty and she said, 'Well, stop the car!'

"We drove on and finally got a discussion going on it, and watched the light. The light continued, so finally after about twenty minutes, we stopped. We got out of the car and looked at what this light was. It appeared to be a flying craft of some sort. It appeared to be hovering up off the road about—well, it was hard to tell because it was about a quarter of a mile back. It seemed to be approximately one hundred feet high off the road. But at that distance, it's hard to tell. You could actually see a wide band of light going around the craft. Then it began operating in a kind of dot-dash fashion—almost like Morse code. We remarked to each other, 'Well...gee...that's odd.'

"So we get our flashlight out and kind of played with this thing, matching it flash for flash. Again, it just stayed there. It just sat there flashing in that odd manner. It was completely silent. Not a sound came from it that we could hear. After doing that for awhile, we said, 'Well, okay, let's get back in the car and see if it follows us.' So we get back in the car and went on down the road a little more. We speeded up—it speeded up; we slowed down—it slowed down.

"Finally, we stopped again. By now we were fifty or sixty miles outside of Dunsmuir. We discussed it and decided it was too late to turn back now. So we just kept going. The craft followed us for another ten or twenty miles and then it just disappeared.

"We went on into Susanville. The last thirty or forty miles we didn't have a drop of gas left in the tank, but somehow we made it. We pulled in at a gas station outside of Susanville. The young man who pumped our gas said he had had several experiences like ours involving strange lights. We then went to a restaurant for breakfast. While we were sitting there it started to get light out. The sun was coming up. We hadn't been watching the time—and suddenly, we realized that three and a half hours were missing!"

A few days after the incident, Erika discovered that there were scars on the insides of both of her ankles. She said that the scars had not been there before the night the craft had followed them between Dunsmuir and Susanville.

Where were Erika and Leda during those missing three and a half hours? What might have transpired during that time? This is a classic missing-time case involving UFO contactees/abductees.

CHAPTER 11

UFO Sightings

U FOs are serious business. Nothing regarding them should be ignored, however trivial the detail might seem. The general reaction to UFO incidents is often scorn and ridicule, particularly from the media, which makes it all the more difficult to find meaningful answers to serious questions.

For example, as I begin writing this chapter (October 10, 1989) a Russian UFO incident is being heavily publicized worldwide. It is the purported landing of a spaceship in a municipal park in the Soviet city of Voronezh. According to a small crowd of witnesses, the UFO circled the park several times and then landed. Minutes later twelve-feet-tall humanoid creatures emerged accompanied by a three-feet-tall robot. According to witnesses, a small boy was hit and temporarily rendered invisible by some sort of beam that shot out from the craft.

The four from the ship then went for a short "promenade" around the park. They then returned to their ship and flew away, while the ship quickly transformed into a shining ball of light as it disappeared into the distance.

The landing, which may be authentic, never received a chance for serious study because of the automatic, worldwide ridicule from the assorted media. The Soviets stuck resolutely by the story, while the Western press had a wonderful time ballyhooing the event as just another screwball flying saucer story—in other words, a joke. After reading the rollicking account of the landing written and carried by the Associated Press, few readers could take the story seriously.

I am confident that some benevolent extraterrestrials wishing to help are becoming thoroughly disgusted with us. They have made overture after overture to us in subtle and sometimes blatant ways, but are again and again rebuffed. Evidence of landings and contacts are greeted by the majority of people with the same disbelief and scorn as the media. What is it finally going to take?

During my information-gathering activities for this book and my previous book, *Mysteries of Sedona*, I came into contact with women and men from all over the world in all walks of life. One thing in particular never ceases to impress me deeply every time it occurs, and that is when I meet someone in a high position of responsibility who takes UFOs and ETs and associated phenomena with an attitude of dead seriousness. Among such individuals I have dealt with are police officers, high-ranking military officers, commercial airline pilots, university professors, psychologists, medical doctors, Ph.D.s in many fields, lawyers, executives with major corporations, famous entertainers, military intelligence officers, engineers, scientists, clergymen and more. Last but certainly not least are hundreds of working stiffs who relentlessly grind out a weekly/monthly subsistence (the author included).

Twenty or thirty years ago many if not most of these very same people would have heartily scoffed at the mere mention of aliens from space, UFOs or flying saucers. The reason for the shift in attitude is that these individuals have had some sort of very real personal experience, one that had great impact and could not be easily explained away.

I was interviewed not long ago by an Austrian journalist. He put a question to me that could apply to most of the UFO/ET/New Age movement in all its forms: "How do you prove any of this stuff to a skeptic?" The obvious answer, of course, is that you don't. A person has to have had some kind of direct, eye-opening, convincing personal experience to be transformed overnight from a devout scoffer to a devout believer.

I have had moments of great glee when someone who had previously regarded me as more than slightly crazy rushed up to me and exclaimed, wide-eyed, with hand on my arm, "My God! I have got to tell you what happened to me last night!" (or yesterday, last week, etc.).

*

The following UFO sightings are some I have accumulated over the past two years.

A woman who lives in an undeveloped, outlying section of Sedona was in her kitchen preparing dinner one evening, when suddenly the entire area surrounding her house was bathed in a dazzling deep-orange color. She rushed out to her back porch in time to see a glowing, disc-shaped object moving north slowly and silently over her house. The object was larger than her house and only a few hundred feet off the ground. She studied it as it followed a deep arroyo below her house—until the disc abruptly "switched off."

*

In the early evening of December 19, 1986, a Sedona man, his wife and two children were driving toward Doe Mountain, which is a flat-topped mesa that stands by itself in the desert a quarter mile past Fay Canyon. They noticed an odd-looking helicopter flying over the top of Doe Mountain. As they watched, a searchlight beamed from the "helicopter," lighting up the top of the expansive mountain.

They stopped the car to get a closer look. They could see that the white "searchlight" turned a crimson red as it came into contact with the surface of the mountain. Then moments later, to their stunned surprise, the "helicopter" exploded into a myriad of Fourth of July-like colors, taking on the shape of a ball. The colorful sphere then rocketed skyward, expanding as it went. Then in an instant it narrowed to a point. They said that for only a second the skyrocketlike fireworks display took on the shape of an enormous spear. A point of brighter light at the tip of the spear flashed once, flashed once again, and then the point of light shot through the clouds at incredible speed.

Several years ago the same Sedona man, while alone one night, heard a sound in the distance that prompted him to dash outside at 1:00 a.m. Approaching him from a distance of about three miles was what he described as a "flying wing." The wing was traveling toward him at a relatively slow speed with the tip, or end of the wing pointed in his direction. Thus he was able to observe it clearly and carefully.

He described it as having multicolored lights in various patterns on the lower surface. He estimated the "wing" size to be from one-quarter to as much as one-half mile in length. The trailing end (or broader part) of the wing evidently contained the propulsion unit. He remarked that the trailing end of the ship was glowing and incandescent. It left in its wake a gradually dissipating vaporous trail of glowing particles. As it passed over his position, it was making the same deep humming sound that had drawn him outside.

Another event, concurrent to this incident, was the sighting of a boomerang-shaped craft that hovered over the town of Morenci, Arizona. It resembled, particularly in size, the UFO the Sedona man had seen. The Morenci UFO hovered over the town in a stationary position long enough for almost the entire population to get a good look at it. The Morenci incident was worldwide front-page news.

*

Over the last thirty years I have seen more than my share of strange objects in the sky. The following three occurrences are among them.

This sighting occurred recently, on September 14, 1989. I had pulled into my driveway when I noticed an orb of orange/white light dipping behind the Mingus Mountains twenty miles to the south. I estimated the object to be twenty-five miles away over an unpopulated area of the Chino Valley behind the Mingus Mountains.

I reached behind the front seat of my van, pulled out my binoculars and focused them on the object. As the ball of orange light went behind the mountains, I saw that it had an almost electric, ice-blue aura surrounding it. I might not have bothered to write about this sighting except for one thing that makes it quite notable. As I stood there in the dark to see if anything else would happen, six of what I think were military jet fighters, spaced one minute apart, came from the precise direction where I had last seen the orb of light.

The jets were flying extremely fast and none of them had on either their strobe lights or their running lights. At the same time, a commercial airliner with all of its navigation lights on flew over, headed in the same direction but at a slightly higher altitude. (Several major commercial airline routes pass over Sedona.)

*

One Thursday in March 1989 I was driving back from Phoenix about 3:00 in the afternoon. I had been in Phoenix for three difficult days and was extremely fatigued. I was driving north on Interstate 17 in an area I learned later was a zone of frequent UFO sightings and in the same general area of the Bill Lewis abduction recounted in Chapter 10. I believe the altered state I was in due to my fatigue was a factor that enabled me to observe what I did.

I was watching what I thought was a single-engine aircraft in the distance. There was something odd about the plane. It was the way it moved. It flew with too smooth a fluidity. It was also painted entirely white, and the white was somehow too bright, as though it were glowing. As the craft began to bank to the north, I thought I would see the expected configuration of a light plane. But to my mounting surprise, when the "plane" banked, it revealed an oval shape—not wings and a tail! Seconds later, before I had a chance to think about it, it flew *behind* a range of mountains five miles away. At that point I was shocked by the realization of the immense size of the UFO. I thought I had been watching a small plane *between* where I was and a distant mountain range. On a later trip, and on passing the same viewpoint from the highway, I carefully estimated the size of the UFO to have been at least several hundred yards in diameter!

✳

At the age of 22, while still living in Maine, I observed on three consecutive nights a red ball of light that looked like a flying road flare. It was maneuvering in and out of a forest near our house. The terrain sloped down and away from our house, and the object appeared to be about a mile away. The UFO was perhaps thirty feet in diameter and moved through the night sky as if it were methodically and purposefully looking for something. On the third night it settled to earth in a grove of maple trees very near a major power line. Even though I maintained a vigil for four more hours that night, I did not see the UFO again.

There is an odd feature that seems to occur often in connection with UFO sightings. This was brought to my attention by a friend in New York State who has had a number of UFO sightings herself. During times of heavy UFO sightings and activity, cars can often be seen at night with only one headlight working. A small thing, but noteworthy. Might it be that there is some sort of unknown energy generated by UFOs (it might *not* be electromagnetic) that affects an automobile's electrical circuitry? An example of this is the following incident.

A Florida woman and her husband, who moved to Sedona in 1987, both have had a series of UFO experiences. The incidents began in Florida and continue in Sedona. This particular Sedona UFO experience was also witnessed by a visitor from Virginia, who has also had some remarkable UFO experiences herself.

This trio had driven up to the Mogollon Rim at the top of Schnebly Hill to watch the sun set over the red rock country. (Schnebly Hill Road is a steep, unpaved road rising to an elevation of 6,500 feet and is an area of notable and consistent UFO sightings.) They were about halfway down the five-mile hill when the car lights abruptly failed. However, the engine continued to operate normally. The three passengers then became aware of a brightly illuminated triangular-shaped UFO, which was hovering silently four or five hundred feet above and to the right of the car.

They watched the craft for five or six minutes, until it disappeared from sight around a towering rock column a half-mile to the west. I carefully questioned the woman about missing time. They were quite knowledgeable on UFO matters, and she stated with assurance that not a minute had been lost. The car operated normally once the UFO was out of sight.

Triangular-shaped UFOs, at least from my findings, seem to be associated with the most sinister of all UFO encounters. It would be most interesting to know who these beings are, where they are from and what their purpose here is. I strongly suspect they are the "Whitley Strieber" types, but they may be of a lower, less evolved species of that race.

In an earlier UFO sighting, this same couple were with a small group that had gone out to Fay Canyon to meditate. They were all looking forward to enjoying the solitude of the desert evening and had just settled down to meditate when a member of the group called everyone's attention to the summit of Bear Mountain, which overlooks Fay Canyon. Their attention was riveted by two large balls of light descending through canyons from the 7,000-foot peak of Bear Mountain. As the lights drew close, they noticed that they were accompanied by smaller lights, which "looked like a swarm of bees flying around the larger lights." The clustered spheres of light then dropped down out of sight into the back of Fay Canyon.

*

In another Sedona-area UFO sighting, three local women recently observed a slow-moving, hat-shaped, grayish-silver UFO fly directly over the municipal airport. It then flew over the town and disappeared behind 6,000-foot Capitol Butte.

In November 1989 two local men sighted a glowing, low-flying object from downtown Sedona at 4:00 a.m. The UFO passed southeast of the city. The two men, who were both working at the time, estimated the UFO's speed to be in excess of 10,000 mph.

In July 1988 a Sedona woman watched from her living-room window in the exclusive Les Springs development an orb of white light zigzag from one point to another to the left of Steamboat Rock, which is one mile west of Schnebly Hill.

In the spring of 1989 two out-of-town visitors watched a blazing white UFO fly over Schnebly Hill from their hotel room in uptown Sedona. They said the UFO stopped high over Schnebly Hill and a glowing, heretofore-unseen red UFO either detached from or flew out of the larger white UFO and repositioned itself seven times in different places around the white UFO. The red UFO then reattached itself to the white UFO, which then flew away at great speed.

Four tourists in the fall of 1988 were hiking on Bell Rock when they observed three disc-shaped UFOs flying in formation over Bell Rock. The UFOs then flew over Apache Mountain to the west. I was informed that one of the tourists took excellent photos of the UFOs.

At 1:00 a.m. one winter night in 1989 two Sedona women were returning from an evening engagement when they saw a UFO traveling very slowly beneath a full moon. They said that from their vantage the UFO was one quarter the size of the moon. Although they said that they had no idea of the actual distance to the ship, they thought the ship to be of an absolutely colossal size. The light of the moon was reflecting smoothly off the ship as the craft passed beneath the moon. The ship, they said, seemed to be a dull, velvety silver color.

As they gazed at the ship, it accelerated at a fantastic rate. In an instant it became elongated into a mercurial silvery shape perhaps several hundred miles long. Then, just as quickly, it vanished.

Late on an afternoon in 1986, a father and son were on Airport Mesa (near the municipal airport) in Sedona enjoying the view of the red rock canyonlands. There had been thunderstorms earlier, and the sky was filled with towering stratocumulus clouds. The ten-year-old boy pointed out a large, silvery, cigar-shaped object that was hanging stationary between the clouds. The object was perfectly backlit by a thunderhead drifting up behind it. They watched the hovering ship for over ten minutes. It remained in the same position until it was obscured by approaching clouds.

A Cottonwood woman was driving alone across Mingus Mountain above Jerome early one morning in 1986. She was stunned by an unexpected sight. To her left and far below, down through a canyon came a procession of fast-moving orange balls of light. Right on their heels were three military helicopters that she said were of the Vietnam type (Hueys). She said the whole thing happened in only ten or eleven seconds.

About the time of the Mingus Mountain occurrence another Cottonwood woman watched a formation of six UFOs position themselves over a power-company substation near the city of Cottonwood. After several minutes they began to move and flew away in a southerly direction.

A man who was asleep in his camper near Fay Canyon awoke one night to find himself unable to move, though perfectly conscious. The entire area around his camper was lit up as if a car with its headlights on high beam was suspended above him. After that he remembers nothing until he woke up at daybreak.

This next UFO incident is unique, even among a collection of incidents already filled with numerous astonishing accounts. I have heard of no other UFO encounter that is identical to this one. It concerns a red-and-white UFO. Because this same red-and-white UFO has been sighted by a half-dozen different individuals at different times, I have no reason to doubt this man's credibility. I shall call him Stan.

His experience was in the area of Loy Butte, in precisely the same area of the story in Chapter 6 of the abduction of Frank Ramsey. Stan was living in a converted schoolbus in the desert near Loy Butte, and on different occasions he had sighted a red-and-white UFO flying nearby at night. This time, however, instead of flying away from where he was, the UFO flew toward him. It came to within easy viewing distance—then stopped. Stan could see that the UFO was large, and had a red bubblelike light underneath. As he gazed at the strange spectacle, the red light detached itself from the bottom of the ship and flew toward him. The red ball of light slowed and slowly circled above Stan and his schoolbus home as if it were looking him over. It circled a number of times and then flew back to the much larger white UFO—which then flew away to the west.

In the fall of 1989, about 8:30 one evening, a Cottonwood-area woman, who was alone in her house, began to hear a highly unusual buzzing sound. The buzzing sound continued, so she went around the house turning off all electrical appliances. Even after she turned everything off, the eerie buzzing sound continued. Then she realized that the sound must be coming from somewhere *outside* of the house. She cautiously went to a window and parted a venetian blind and peeked out.

In the sky over her house she saw five sets of stationary red lights hovering over the house. She says, mysteriously, that she lost about an hour of time that evening that she can't account for.

*

A local woman was hiking in Long Canyon in December 1989, and in a narrow area where I have recorded a number of strange events. This particular event happened to her: She was walking along a trail when a large manzanita bush (5 feet high by 10 feet wide) began to shake violently. She said that the wind was not blowing and no cows were scratching themselves on the other side of the bush. She walked two-thirds of the way around the bush, but nothing was near the bush and bushes around it were perfectly quiet. The bush was still shaking violently as she walked away down the trail.

*

The following incident is another one of mysterious nocturnal lights: A Sedona woman was staying over with friends one evening. She was asleep on the couch when she was awakened after midnight. In the kitchen window was a brilliant reddish-orange light. The light from this bright object bathed the room.

Suddenly, from the two separate bedrooms came voices talking in a language she had never heard. The strange voices seemed to be talking to each other—then she realized it was her two sleeping friends who were speaking in this strange language. The woman on the couch tried to get up to get a tape recorder, but found that she was immobilized from the neck down. Moments later, she strangely fell asleep. Over the next few weeks the incident slowly returned to her conscious memory.

*

Regarding the next incident, I know of four others similar to this that occurred in the same general neighborhood. In this particular case, a Florida couple was asleep when they awoke early in the morning, about 2 a.m.

An orange orb of light drifted into their room. The man said in a matter-of-fact tone "They're here," as if he may have been in a semiconscious state. The next day the woman had a bothersome nosebleed in *both* nostrils.

After returning to Florida, the woman, convinced that something quite odd had occurred that night, underwent hypnosis. The doctor who performed the hypnosis was well qualified, as he had once headed the psychology department of one of the world's most prestigious universities.

Under hypnosis it was revealed that the woman found herself in a brightly lit room illuminated by blue-white lights, where many faces with huge eyes stared down at her. There was a "fuzzy-feeling" collar around her neck, and something was exerting pressure into the back of her head and neck. The first hypnosis session was too alarming for her and so was cut short. She may, perhaps later, allow a deeper probe into the incident.

As she left the doctor's office she experienced intense pain in both left and right sinuses, in the upper nostril area.

*

Last are the following two entries in this collection of UFO sightings. These involve something that has become more and more common lately—glowing green UFOs.

Not long ago a husband and wife were looking toward Sedona from the east. They were discussing an odd and enormous egg-shaped cloud sitting high over the town. They were remarking about its almost perfect symmetry when three large globes of green light dropped from the bottom of the cloud and sped away in three different directions.

Several months ago a close friend reported glancing out her bedroom window at 11:00 p.m. on a July evening. She looked out in time to see a green sphere of light streak cometlike across the sky and disappear in an arc *behind the trees* in the area of Fay Canyon and Doe Mountain.

One possible explanation for the number of UFO/ET incidents in the Sedona area are the world-famous energy vortexes that are located here. Are "they" here because of the energy generated by these powerful vortexes? The majority of UFO sightings are indeed in the general area of these mysterious energy fields.

CHAPTER 12

Lila Lee Underwood

This is one woman's remarkable story of direct physical contact, in a most positive way, with both human extraterrestrials and humanoid extraterrestrials. In her own words:

"My introduction to the extraterrestrial beings came about in a most unusual way through these following incidents.

"I felt strangely led to a particular lot on the north side of Dayton, Ohio. My family had always lived in Dayton, and I was looking for land on which to build a family home. There was no 'for sale' sign on the property that I was drawn to, but I found that the owner was willing to sell two acres to me for the ridiculously low price of $1500. This in spite of the fact that the going price across the street was $6000 *per half acre*! I bought the land. A few days later, while getting estimates from lumber companies, I felt compelled to compare prices with a business that sold precut lumber homes.

"Three days later I ran into a friend who remarked, 'I went by your lot yesterday, and I see that you have an excavation dug for your house.'

"'No, I don't,' I replied.

"'Yes you do,' she insisted.

"So I went out to see for myself...and there it was!

"That particular precut-homes company I had visited had advertised free excavations to anyone who bought a house from them, but I hadn't signed for one, so I went back to talk to them. They apologized profusely when they found found out what had happened, and they asked me if I would accept the excavation at no cost. I had planned to have one dug anyway, so of course I said yes.

"A few days later while driving around getting cost estimates on building materials, the same friend saw me and said, 'I drove by your property yesterday and I see that you've had your building material delivered.'

"'No, I haven't,' I said.

"'Yes you have,' she said.

"So I went back to the property and there neatly stacked on my lot was everything necessary to build a house. The precut-homes people had struck again.

"I immediately drove to the office of the company and asked one of the salesman if they had delivered all that material. He didn't know; however, he went in search of their foreman to find out. The foreman said they had delivered it.

"I was amazed. 'Look,' I said, very perturbed, 'I haven't signed anything and I haven't ordered anything. I don't even know if your delivery is the kind of building materials I need.'

"Then they started to give me the runaround. Nobody wanted to talk to me, nobody wanted to take the blame. So I became very angry. It was Sunday afternoon and they were crowded with customers, so I stood in the middle of their model home and shouted, 'Do you mean to tell me this is the way you do business?' And went on shouting about the whole affair. This got everyone's undivided attention. The owner rushed out, grabbed me by the arm and hustled me into his office. They ended up giving everything to me, at their cost, from roofing to nails. And then they closed the deal by adding, 'If you need anything else to finish the job, come and get it.' They even sent a crew over to help me get started. Surprisingly (or maybe not so surprisingly), the excavation and building materials were almost exactly what I needed to build my house.

"While the house was under construction, there was much UFO activity over the forest in back of the construction site. Late one night one of these ships landed on a knoll behind the unfinished house. A neighbor woman said that its flashing red lights, reflecting on her bedroom walls, woke her during the night. She was startled and thought at first that it was the police bringing her son home, that he must have done something wrong. She stayed in bed and waited, but the doorbell didn't ring, and the lights kept flashing. Finally she got up and looked out her bedroom window and saw pulsating red lights emanating from a large, silvery disc. She noticed much strange activity going on around my place. Mesmerized, she watched this for about three hours, she said. She wasn't sure what was going on. Then while she was away from the window the UFO disappeared. The next day when I arrived at the construction site, I found a burned-out circle in the grass that measured 30 feet in diameter. I went to talk to the neighbor woman, and she quickly told me what she had seen the night before.

"After we had moved into the house I began almost immediately to be interested in metaphysical books. I became a compulsive seeker for 'truth'; I also learned how to meditate in the Eastern way. Then late one night shortly after moving, I had strange visitors. My husband and our children were asleep. I was in the living room reading and meditating. I looked up and saw two small entities entering through closed patio doors. They were very pale, almost white, had large heads with no hair, huge black wraparound beetle eyes and small, childlike bodies with long, skinny arms and thin legs. They were dressed in skin-tight metallic jumpsuits made from shiny, silvery fishscale material that didn't wrinkle when they moved. I wasn't at all frightened by them. They seemed very kind and gentle. When I looked into their eyes it was as if we were one. I felt myself being drawn into their eyes; it was as if I could fall right into them. In them I found that I knew new dimensions of wisdom and love. And I knew I could trust them. They were the Strieber ET types, but this was long before I knew about Whitley Strieber. This was in 1969. We spoke telepathically, as easily as if we were speaking aloud. They said they recognized the work that I had been doing spiritually: clairaudiently receiving spiritual lessons, teaching metaphysical groups, doing energy healing, counseling and healing grieving children on the astral plane who had died. Then they asked if I would go with them and work with them. I agreed to go.

"They took me to what appeared to be a laboratory in their ship. The walls of this round room were lined with banks of computerlike machines. In the center of the room stood a solid, white, rectangular block table that looked like marble and that somehow collected data on anything placed upon it and transferred that data to the ship's computers. I was instructed to lie on the table. I thought it would be cold and hard, but it was quite comfortable, for as I laid on it I found myself floating just above it. I don't know what happened next, as I didn't remember anything else until I was ready to come home. It was the same with each successive visit. From the beginning, they became nightly visitors and I always went with them, traveling sometimes in my body and sometimes traveling in the astral body.

"So much was happening during this time. My whole life was being changed. My mind was being expanded. I was cognizant that I was being advanced carefully in consciousness awareness, step by step. I was introduced in time to an ascended master teacher who was with me constantly and who taught me much. I then used these same lessons to teach my own classes. Later I taught by channeling the lessons directly from the master to them. It was quality work; the lessons were excellent. I did this for about a year. It seemed to be one of the steps in my development. Later on I was taken one more step: to consciously channel directly from my God self.

"At about this time, as another step in my spiritual development, my master teacher took me to the akashic level to meet one who was introduced to me as the Lord of Records. He appeared ancient, had long white hair and wore a white robe. He took me to the Hall of Records and brought out my Book of Life. He handed it to me opened to that present time in my life. It was a large, metallic-gold book, and by flipping back through it I found all of my past lives, many that I remembered. Then by turning ahead I could also read about my future. It was fascinating. As I had begun to read of my future, he took the book from me and said, 'Now, Lila, do this for others.' I was confused. I wondered how I would ever do this for others, but I shouldn't have. I should've known my wise mentors would arrange for me to read the akashic records. This is how it happened.

"A week or so after meeting the Lord of Records, a friend called me and asked if I would help her with a charity party to raise money to furnish a new hospital wing. I said I would. It was to be a psychic party, she added, and they had invited psychics from three states. When I got there, the large parking lot was filled with cars. There were people lined up inside the halls and lined up into the parking lot outside the door. As I went in, my friend rushed over to me and exclaimed, 'Oh, Lila! I'm so glad you're here. *NONE OF THE PSYCHICS SHOWED UP! You're it!'*

"I was aghast. 'Oh, no! I've never done this. I can't!'

"She answered resolutely, 'We are not giving their money back. Get in there and do it.' Then while I was still bewildered she shoved me into a little room furnished with a card table and two chairs. And there I was.

"She told me confidently not to worry. 'It's a party,' she said. 'Just say something off the top of your head and make up funny stuff.'

"I sat there wondering what to do. Then they started coming in. The first person asked, 'Do I have cancer?' The next one asked, 'Is my daughter on drugs?' And the next one, 'Is my husband running around on me?'

"I prayed desperately. 'Oh, God! Help me!' And immediately I began to hear and see the answers just as I had before in the akashic level. I was reading the life records of these people.

"I worked for almost five hours before I had to stop from sheer exhaustion, but at the same time I was exhilarated. I still don't know how I drove home. I think I must have floated. I'm sure the ETs had set this all up for me to entice me to begin my psychic counseling work. Most of these people called back later saying, 'Lila, you helped so much in the few minutes we had together, will you work with me more?' And the word spread by mouth and continues even now.

"Another step in this unusual training occurred during that same span of time. I was working with the ETs, when I was taken into the presence of a council of ascended masters...

"I had prayed for a certain amount of money to pay a bill and I had heard that I would have it. So when the time came and I didn't have it, I prayed again: 'Lord, you told me that when the time came that I would need it, I would have the money. It's time now and I don't have it. What happened?' An astonishing thing then transpired. I began to see a circle of white-robed beings, and they were discussing my prayer.

"'She's right,' someone said, 'we told her that. What have you done?' questioned one to another.

"Came the answer, 'Me? I didn't know it was my job!'

"'Well, we'd better do something now because it *is* time,' they said.

"I couldn't believe what I was seeing and hearing...Was I going crazy? Here was an ethereal council, deliberating over my prayer. Usually when I prayed, I saw and heard Christ answer, and on rare occasions I heard God speak. This was not at all the same.

"I was still questioning whether I was crazy or not, when that afternoon my doorbell rang and a young man (human ET?) stood there with an envelope that contained the exact amount of money I needed—$438.23.

"Their counsel continued every time I prayed—and I just listened. I never interrupted them or said anything, until about six months later when I heard them talking about something that I knew about which they evidently didn't. I overcame my timidity and said, 'Excuse me, have you considered...?' There was immediate shocked silence, and they simply withdrew into a higher dimension. I realized then that they hadn't known I could see and hear them.

"A year passed before I had any known contact with them again. Then they returned and allowed me to join them. They said, 'You may be here with us, but don't say anything.' I felt like a junior member. Several years later I was allowed to come into this etheric council as a full member, and now we work together counseling others (see bibliography).

"Evidence of other-worldly beings in my life continued. There was the time an unearthly foreign language spoken in a whispery male voice came onto my audio tape. I had been meditating prior to putting a lesson on cassette tape that was to be used by my class while I was away. As I came out of meditation, I turned the tape on and let it run a few minutes before I began to speak. Later when I replayed the tape an eerie voice filled what I had thought would be quiet, empty space. I asked for an interpretation of the foreign message and heard, 'We are looking for people who will work with us to help enlighten human beings, and who will help to bring peace to the Earth.'

"I answered that I would work with anyone who worked in the spirit of Christ. Later when we replayed the tape again, the second word spoken by the whispery voice, which sounded like 'croos,' had been changed to the word 'Christ.'

"...Or there was the time when beautiful angelic singing manifested on a woman's tape while I counseled her.

"And on three different occasions miraculous physical interventions occurred that have literally saved my life during dangerous traffic or road conditions.

"In a similar but unrelated event, when I was hiking with a friend, I felt an unseen presence on the trail. I greeted it and invited it to come onto my photos. Immediately a blue light began to appear and it moved ahead of us, playfully peeking out from behind the rocks at us. Later it expanded to a great size that filled the upper part of a cave, and then dropped down to cover an ancient Indian ruin in the cave.

"In still another incident I saw flashes of lightning in a clairvoyant vision one morning while I was receiving a lesson from Christ. That evening, while teaching that lesson to my group in Ohio, lightning flashed outside every time I spoke Christ's name. I paused after the third lightning bolt and asked the group, 'Are you noticing what is happening?' This continued for about 30 minutes until the lesson was finished.

"I believe all of these incredible events are somehow directly tied up with my work with the ETs. My specific work with them went on nearly every night for approximately 18 months. At the end of that period I had a different type of ET visitor. He came into my home one evening when I was alone, in the same manner as the others had come. But this fellow appeared to be human. He was a little over average height, of slight build, and he looked a lot like the young man that had delivered the money to me from the council. He was very handsome, dressed in a grey business suit and tie. Telepathically he conveyed this thought, 'Lila, you've been so cooperative and helpful. We'd like to do something for you as a reward. Will you come with me?' I felt a genuine warmth and kindness in his invitation and it felt good to be appreciated. I agreed to go.

"He took my hand, and we dematerialized in the usual way I had grown accustomed to through working nightly with the ETs: the room started to disappear around us, then in an instant everything went gray and immediately there was the feeling of traveling very fast. As we materialized again, I began to see the new surroundings. We were on the streets of a fashionable residential section of a large city. It was twilight time and there were other people on the streets too. We walked for quite a long distance through an area of attractive homes, and then after awhile we came to a slum area. I began to be frightened and I heard my guide speaking in my mind, 'There is no need to be frightened, Lila. We are almost there.'

"We stopped walking finally, and came to a large brick warehouse that had all of its windows boarded up. We stood before old wooden double doors large enough for a semi truck to drive through. My guide knocked on the door. There was a hole in the door, with what looked like a board covering it on the inside. We saw the board move and someone looked out at us, and one of the doors opened.

"We went in, and there inside this cavernous old building was a huge disc-shaped craft. There were tiny workmen dressed in silvery jumpsuits working on it. One little workman in particular was standing high up on a motorized dolly platform. I picked up his thoughts. He was thinking, 'I've done this, and I've done that, and I've done this other thing...and nothing works!' He was getting very upset because, I felt, he didn't want to come down and talk to the supervisor. But he realized he must, so he pushed the buttons on his dolly and started coming down to ground level. About that time another ET, who seemed to be in charge, was sitting at a desk looking at plans and knew we had entered. He turned and walked toward us. As he came across the room I heard him telepathically ask my guide, 'Do we have to talk to her verbally or can she hear us?' 'Oh, she can hear you all right,' my guide said. Then the little worker, who had come down to ground level on the dolly, stopped the supervisor, and with one sigh, transferred all of his exasperated thoughts about his fruitless efforts. The supervisor looked into his eyes, and in one mental instant showed him the plans, gave him a detailed explanation of what was wrong, and told him exactly how to fix it. The worker climbed back onto the platform of his dolly, rose to the level he needed to be on, and shortly after exclaimed, 'Yes! It works!'

"My guide then turned to me and said, 'Lila, have you seen enough, or do you want to stay longer?' I felt that the supervisor, who was standing there with us, was 'all business' and that he didn't really want to waste any more time with us.

"I looked around and thought for a moment, then replied, 'I think we're in the way. We'd better leave.'

"We traveled back to my home in the same way we had come. I was sure we had been at the warehouse in our bodily forms. I had seen people looking at us on the streets, and occasionally stepping out of our way as we walked by.

"A few days later someone I hardly knew called to invite me to lunch to meet a visiting friend of hers from Washington, D.C. I felt I had to accept. As we talked I found out her friend was a psychic hired by our government. I thought she might know something about the warehouse, so I told her about what I had seen. She said without hesitation, 'Oh, yes, I know all about that. That building is in Boston. In fact, the government gave that warehouse to them. We try to cooperate with them however and whenever we can.'

"Occasionally I see UFOs in the sky and we communicate. Those that are unfriendly don't respond. I'm not afraid of them. I know there is a universal law that no one can harm those who are associated with Christ and the Great White Brotherhood. We have their protection. One time I heard, 'Don't worry, Lila, before things get too bad on Earth, you'll be abducted.' I didn't like that word, abducted, and said so, but they repeated the word, 'abducted.' I understand now that there will be a mass evacuation soon and I'm glad I know the abductors.

"I didn't have any more personal contact with the ETs until I moved to Sedona. I had felt compelled to move here, as if I had waited all my life to find this 'home.' Then one day, after hiking about in the red rocks, as I came into my empty apartment (my furniture hadn't arrived yet) and stepped into my bedroom, there stood a little ET, without his silvery suit. I was so happy to see him.

He held out his skinny long arms to me and we hugged, and it was like being hugged by universal love. His little body felt soft, like a baby's body. I couldn't let go. We hugged for several minutes, then I suppose it was too difficult for him to maintain a physical form any longer without his suit, so he began to dematerialize...and he was gone."

CHAPTER 13

Paranormal Encounters

In earlier chapters I spoke of a fourth level of entities, which I call interdimensionals, or ultraterrestrials. A few, but not all, of the following incidents fall squarely into that category of high-strangeness, interdimensional activity. The more I delve into the field of UFO study, the more I run across accounts that seem to be attributable to these exotic life forms. I have a driving interest to get to the bottom of this particular phenomenon, and with luck and a lot of help, perhaps I will.

I am aware that other camps of metaphysical opinion refer to certain entities of a highly mysterious nature by such names as incubi, succubae, jinns, ahrimanes, illuminatus, etc. We may be talking about the same thing, but I prefer to deviate from such antiquated terminology with its Dark Ages connotation, and use more modern terms like interdimensional and ultraterrestrial. No matter what the terminology, from this level can come some strange critters indeed!

Some of the beings of this ultraterrestrial category can take physical form. To them it may be a relatively simple matter of rearranging their molecular/cellular structure. By many estimations (and certainly not just mine) there are thousands of alien beings of divergent origins living and working among us as clerks, bus drivers, typists, school teachers, factory workers, politicians, college students—all the occupations. The latest statistics show that the average American spends 7 hours a day watching television, or about 45 hours a week—is it any wonder that extraterrestrial aliens have little problem moving among us unseen?

The question is, *why?* Why do they need to infiltrate humanity? What is their reason or goal? Think of some of the people you have met in the past that just didn't fit. They seemed to be different somehow—and maybe they were!

As I have written in other works, we must stretch our thinking and make the greatest effort to try to understand them and their brand of reality. Our small chunk of reality may not fit at all into the universal reality that most other life forms adhere to. Are we the mavericks—the oddballs? Perhaps they have come to try to understand how we have made it this long. Or are we a bunch of misfits from elsewhere, confined here to learn and to squabble and fight amongst ourselves in a remote part of space where we will do the least damage? The Earth is a schoolroom all right, no question of that—but *why?*

Another possibility: Have we as a race fallen blindly and willingly under a form of indenture to some specific race of extraterrestrials? Is it possible that these same ETs keep us squabbling and quarreling among ourselves and otherwise distracted, so that we don't discover that we have the same awesome powers they have? Could it be that this is all part of a win-or-lose Cosmic Game? Is one of the rules of the game that if we discover the key and stick to it—we win?

Is the "key" a full utilization of the dormant powers we possess so that we can finally be free, and can be as all the other "Gods" of the Universe who have attained a specific level of enlightenment and now are truly free?

I have lived in Sedona nearly three years, and occasionally I will meet someone who has seen the "Little People." Although I have had little experience with this level of super reality, I feel it is worthy of inclusion here. These beings, when sighted, usually are of the leprechaun or elf type—short, squat, human-looking little beings who are often colorfully dressed. They disappear in the wink of an eye.

One could easily discount Little People stories as merely a childish flight of romantic fantasy or a way to escape day-to-day pressures—except that these Little People have been reported all over the world from the beginning of the written word. They never seem to do any harm, but just go about minding their own business, with perhaps a little playful mischief now and then.

In my opinion, there is solid proof of the existence of the Little People. See George C. Andrew's book, *Extraterrestrials Among Us,* pages 37-38 (photograph in his illustration section). In October

1932 two gold prospectors were working in a gulch in the Pedro Mountains sixty miles west of Casper, Wyoming. They had located on a gulch wall what looked to be an indication of the presence of gold. So they elected to blast at that spot.

After the smoke had cleared, the two men were astounded to find that the explosion had revealed the entrance to a subterranean cave. When they peered inside, they were even more astounded to discover the mummified corpse of a tiny man sitting on a ledge at the back of the cave.

The little man was later x-rayed and studied by experts from Harvard University, the American Museum of Natural History, the Wyoming State Historical Society, and Boston Museum's Egyptian Department. He was found to have body parts nearly identical to those of a human. The body was fourteen inches tall, weighed twelve ounces, had a full set of teeth, and was about sixty-five years old at death. A scientist named him Hesperopithicus. They have no idea how long ago the little man died, other than their statement that the body was of an extremely great age. Remember, he was entombed in solid rock!

✳

I was recently given a report by a man who is building a home in the sparsely populated Red Canyon/Loy Butte area near Sedona. He told me that one day he had been touring his property when he encountered something that looked like a "window" or portal suspended in midair. Near the portal were several nine-feet-tall Bigfoot-type creatures that were, without question, guarding the portal. The man did not remain long in the area. I have since interviewed another man who had a nearly identical experience in the same general area. These two men do not know each other.

I have a fourth-person account about a local man who was transporting stolen Hopi, Navajo and Apache artifacts from northern Arizona to California to sell. He was driving along at 3:00 a.m. through a long stretch of unpopulated desert when something caught his eye. He caught a motion to his left from the open window. He turned to look, and to his shock, he saw that a very large owl was flying outside the window—looking him squarely in the eyes. According to the story, the man took it as an omen, and shortly after found a different way to make a living!

Many hawk, eagle, raven and owl experiences are no doubt Indian-related. I have recorded some unusual stories of encounters with large birds. These may be directly attributable to Indian guardian spirits, or "protectors."

A Sedona woman has had several uncommon large-bird encounters such as a red-tailed hawk sitting on a tree in her front lawn for an entire day. The Forest Service inspected the bird and declared it to be perfectly healthy.

This same woman and her husband had another experience at the same time as the hawk incident. One day they had an overwhelming urge to go out to the canyons to meditate. They found themselves drawn to an area of privately owned land that was an exceedingly unlikely spot in which to meditate. The woman described the spot to me, and I knew exactly where it is. They had to get permission to meditate there, as it was almost in someone's backyard. Odd, when you consider that in the immediate area are vast, open National Forest lands.

They had meditated for ten or fifteen minutes when suddenly they were aware that they were no longer alone. They opened their eyes and not fifty feet away was an Indian man dressed in white, sitting on a white horse. Recovering from their surprise, they got to their feet and started toward the Indian. The Indian said nothing, but began to move away, keeping a fair distance from the couple. They followed him for over a quarter of a mile. The Indian and the white horse went behind a thicket of small trees—and vanished.

*

I feel the need to emphasize again that stories like this could be easily discounted as some sort of flight of fancy or an illusion, except for the presence of some contributing factor that makes the story credible.

No matter how unusual or bizarre a story sounds, I always file it away for future reference. Thus I have often found that different people in different places and at different times have had some sort of similar or related experience, which then gives the original strange story great credibility.

In this case, what demanded my undivided attention was the fact that the spot where the couple went to meditate is the exact center of an area of recent intense UFO activity. This particular area is about one mile square and has been the scene of some extraordinarily odd paranormal activity.

Another incident I have recorded, unique in itself, is the following. In September 1989 two teenage girls and their mothers had hiked to the top of Steamboat Rock in Oak Creek Canyon. The women were deeply spiritual and of a metaphysical turn, but their two daughters had little interest in such matters. It had been a pleasant but moderately strenuous hike to the summit of Steamboat Rock. Once there, they had enjoyed the spectacular panorama of Sedona, the red rocks and the ramparts of Oak Creek Canyon.

They had begun the trek back down from the top, the two girls keeping a slower pace and staying a considerable distance behind their mothers. They had gone about halfway down the mountain and had entered an area of sparse, stunted pines. The girls were making their way carefully down the steep, rocky trail when they noticed a distinct, shimmering form beginning to take shape nearby in the pine trees.

As the startled girls watched, the finely outlined features of a radiantly beautiful young woman with black hair and angelic features came into full view. One girl was terrified by what she was seeing, but the other girl was nearly overcome with awe by the beauty of what she saw. The angelic apparition made a gesture of friendliness, smiled warmly and then vanished as quickly as she had appeared.

The two girls excitedly told their mothers about what they had experienced. Little more was said about the incident—until a few weeks later during a shopping trip to Flagstaff. While in a store, one of the daughters was drawn to a display of books. She picked up a book that seemed almost to beckon to her. She began to thumb through the book and was stunned when her eyes went to an almost godlike painting of a robed and radiantly beautiful young woman with dark eyes and black hair. It was the same young woman the two girls had seen materialize just weeks earlier on Steamboat Rock!

The painting was of Our Lady of Medjugorje (pronounced Madre Goria), Yugoslavia. Our Lady, also called Mary, has been appearing to crowds of the curious there since 1981. In the last few years she has appeared in several other locations around the world. Along with her appearances come extraordinary, almost psychedelic displays of colors in the sky around the town of Medjugorje. This display is particularly vivid over the barren hill on which she originally made her first appearance to peasants.

The popular belief among those who make the pilgrimage to Medjugorje is that Our Lady is a purely spiritual being, or angel, sent from God. This may be, but interestingly enough, several years ago Our Lady allowed herself to be photographed by a devout follower. Her features are not typically human. Most striking is her unusually narrow chin. Could it be that Our Lady of Medjugorje is an extraterrestrial? One who is trying to gently and compassionately bring about a certain realization to humanity—in a way that humanity can willingly accept, considering its preconceived notions?

In a separate Sedona sighting that is in somewhat the same vein, I received this report from a local man several weeks after the two girls' Steamboat Rock experience. This took place in the Schnebly Hill area, which is only about a mile from Steamboat Rock.

The local man had spent the night with a metaphysical group that had camped on the Mogollon Rim at the top of Schnebly Hill. From that vantage point, you can look down upon an area called the Merry-Go-Round by locals, and upon a lower 80-foot-diameter Indian medicine wheel (rocks arranged in a wagon-wheel formation) placed there in 1987 and used for metaphysical and Indian ceremonial gatherings.

Early in the morning he went to the edge of the Rim and looked down to the medicine wheel. In the medicine wheel were a large number of people dressed in bright white robes. They were standing in a circle inside the medicine wheel. He called excitedly to the others and they rushed over, only to see nothing. They mumbled something about someone not getting enough sleep.

The man, convinced he had not been seeing things, remembered noticing a tent pitched by campers near the area of the medicine wheel. On the drive back to town he stopped his car and walked to where he had seen the tent. Somewhat sheepishly he asked the campers if they had seen a large group of white-robed people standing in a circle in the medicine wheel. Their immediate response was, "You saw that too?"

In 1987 a metaphysical group met in West Sedona. Part of the session was spent discussing UFOs and related activities. The group took a break halfway through the meeting. Suddenly, cries and shouts arose from those who had gone outside on the large deck. Forty people rushed outside to see what the commotion was about. Everyone was pointing excitedly at the sky.

There in the sky for all to see was the word YAHWEH spelled out in the clouds in perfectly formed letters. The clouds that day were long, stringy ones. But YAHWEH was spelled out by great puffy clouds high in the northwestern sky. The incredible display formed quickly and dissipated quickly, but it was seen by every member of the group, about 55 people. By the time cameras were brought out, the last remaining letter, A, was almost gone.

Immediately after the puffy clouds dissipated, three brilliant red points of light appeared over a hilltop a mile away. The red lights remained until dark, then blinked out one by one.

*

In the last few years I have investigated reports of strange lights in the canyons. Essentially this story is described with many variations by different people at different times.

Last spring the local newspaper ran a short story about lights that residents had been seeing in the sky at night. The lights were attributed to a rare combination of aerial phenomena, including the aurora borealis. A number of witnesses described colors of a red/blue or blue shade. The unusual lights were seen in the area of Coffee Pot Rock and Capitol Butte.

According to two of the witnesses, at 11:00 p.m. one night Coffee Pot Rock and Capitol Butte (an area of several square miles) were backlit by what looked like blue floodlights, which occasionally streamed skyward. The only problem with the aurora borealis/northern lights newspaper story is that a man was camping on the Rim that night overlooking the entire Sedona region. He emphatically and resolutely states that he was looking *down* on the red/blue lights. He said they were only in the area of Capitol Butte.

In another incident involving a blue light, a Sedona woman who had just moved here said that late one night as she sat watching TV, a blue ball of light flowed through her front door. This blue light drifted over and completely engulfed her as she sat in the chair—with a mysterious loss of several hours of time resulting.

In 1985 two men, whom I will call Bill and John, had climbed to the summit of Bell Rock. This is a steep, dangerous and difficult climb. Bill and John were on the precipitous summit when John's expensive jacket was blown off the ledge where they were standing by a sudden strong wind. The jacket fell several hundred feet before coming to rest on a projecting rock shelf.

John, a Silicon Valley computer expert, immediately resolved to climb back down, get his fishing rod and try to retrieve his prized jacket. Bill, who is a retired vice president of one of New York's largest corporations, said, "Wait a minute. We are manifestors. Let's have the wind elements blow it back up to us!" John, already starting back down, thought for a moment and replied, "Well, why not, it's worth a try."

The two men meditated intently on the jacket, and minutes later a powerful gust of wind arose. The jacket lifted off the ledge far below and—fell at their feet on the summit of the lofty rock!

Along with the Bell Rock jacket incident, there are three other narratives that may or may not be related. In all three cases, a woman was involved.

These are three totally separate incidents and all three involve individuals climbing on a rock ledge or cliff—and falling off—only to be caught by "something" and deposited back at the point of origin, or on safe ground. Two of these occurred in Boynton Canyon. Although I can't confirm these incidents in any way, they do have a place in the cataloging of unusual happenings here. I certainly wouldn't want to test the theory, but if true, it does reinforce the idea of something extraordinary inhabiting Sedona's canyons.

*

During the course of collecting accounts of paranormal phenomena, one evening I was interviewing a Sedona woman about a series of UFO experiences she had had. She mentioned that she'd had an unusual dream several months before. Normally, dreams don't interest me much, although I do feel that they are meaningful. However, my ears really perked up at this one. As I mentioned earlier, one thing by itself might be relatively meaning-less, but when another factor enters you often suddenly have something of great significance.

The woman said she had experienced an astral-travel dream that seemed so real that she felt she was actually there. She said she had left her body one night while dreaming and saw herself floating over the scrub pine forests of Sedona, going west toward the canyons. In a short time she came to a doorway that led to an underground UFO base. She found herself drifting through this solid portal into the midst of a scene of beehivelike activity. Many humans and nonhuman aliens were busily going about activities that seemed to have great urgency. She said they didn't even notice her—or perhaps were not interested in her presence.

Up to that point I was thinking to myself that it was just an interesting dream—no big deal. Then I asked her to describe the area where she thought the "portal" to be. It turned out that the portal in her dream was in the precise area where I had been conducting my most detailed investigation of UFO activity. She had no way of knowing that. There are hundreds of square miles of forest and canyonlands around Sedona. However, her dream had taken her to the exact location of my ongoing research. I'm still trying to figure that one out!

In October 1989 I spoke on the mysteries of Sedona to a large contingent of metaphysical seekers who were here for a seminar from all parts of the United States and the world. I am always quite reluctant to speak to groups, especially large ones, unless I know exactly what their spiritual experience is and what it is they expect to hear from me.

In this case I found the group to be open-minded and fun. We were having a lively and interesting exchange after my main presentation. I was talking about some of the weird things that go on around here and around the world, when an attractive woman in her early thirties, a Pennsylvania attorney, interrupted me to say that she *had* to tell me what had happened to her the day before. After hearing my talk on paranormal and ET activity, she felt encouraged to talk openly about her own experience.

She said excitedly that she had been out for her daily three-mile run the afternoon before. She had been running at a moderate pace on a gravel road near the county rifle range, when suddenly the sound of running footsteps approached rapidly from behind. She thought another runner had caught up to her—or worse.

She slowed and looked back. There was not a living creature in sight, but still the footfalls persisted and were steadily catching up to her. She was evidently a superb runner, so as the sound of the plodding feet caught up to her, she shifted into an all-out sprint. The footfalls paced her own, stride for stride for only a short distance, then began to drop back. She soon outdistanced the sound of the footfalls—and whatever invisible creature was making them. She said she was sure she did the last mile in world-record time!

These next two paranormal incidents are personal experiences I have had. I am pleased to have the opportunity to present them here.

When I first moved to Sedona I spent a great deal of time in Boynton Canyon. Nearly every day for three months I hiked the two-mile round trip. I have several out-of-the-way places I enjoy going to there. At one spot I and others noticed a twenty-foot by twenty-foot-square indentation on the sheer face of a nearby cliff. It almost looked as if it had been cut square, it was so perfect.

Over the last two years I (we) have watched the profile of an Indian face take shape in the center of this area. The profile started at the forehead, and inch by inch has extended downward and is now a face. The diagram below is an exact replica of what has appeared on the red-rock cliff.

My last entry in this chapter is the account of an experience I had that baffled me for over fifteen years. Until, that is, I began the study of UFOs and related phenomena.

In the spring of 1973 I was driving across the country from California to Maine. I almost always camp out on these trips. I was driving on U.S. Highway 666 between Wilcox and Safford, Arizona.

Looking for a place to camp, I had followed a gravel road off Highway 666 into a remote area of the Pinaleno Mountains. I drove until I found a spot that suited me, with good views and little chance of being disturbed by other campers.

I had been there about an hour and had the camp all set up. It was about 7:00 p.m. In the distance I heard the rattle and clatter of a vehicle coming rather fast. I was surprised to see a battered, rusty yellow Volkswagen Beetle coming up the old mining road. It was coming at a rate of speed I thought was far too fast for the rough, unpaved road. I was standing several hundred feet off the road and was well concealed in a thick grove of yucca plants and a variety of tall cacti.

The VW went by out on the road, trailed by an immense dust cloud. In the front seats were two men with long, dark-brown hair, who appeared to be in their early thirties. I watched the speeding yellow VW go far up into the mountains. The little car remained clearly in sight as it traveled up a broad alluvial fan at the foot of the high mountains.

I began watching the car with my binoculars. Eventually, the VW pulled up to an ancient, corrugated metal mining shack at the end of the road. The two men got out and spent fifteen or twenty minutes walking in and out and around the dilapidated metal shack. I watched them get back into their VW, and the car quickly resumed that reckless rate of speed back down the long, sloping hillside. A tremendous roostertail of dust plumed skyward behind the little speck of yellow.

In minutes I lowered the binoculars, for the yellow car was now easily seen with the naked eye. I was growing uneasy, as I began to suspect that the two men were up to no good. I also knew that from the angle of their present location they could easily see my red pickup with its white camper shell. I was not prepared for what happened next.

The car, going at that breakneck speed, came hurtling down the hill. I could by then hear it as well as see it. The yellow car dipped down into a shallow gully, and for a moment I lost sight of it. I waited, watching. Several seconds went by while I stood looking and waiting for the little car and its two occupants to reappear at the top of the hill. But nothing happened. There was only silence. The mammoth dust cloud caught up to the shallow gully and began to slowly dissipate in the absolute silence of the desert.

A hundred thoughts raced through my mind. I became more and more confused as each minute went by. I knew that at the high speed the car was traveling, even if it had hit something or the driver had locked up the brakes, the momentum of the car would have carried it over the top of that hill. I started to experience panic. I decided they had seen my truck and had somehow stopped. Perhaps at that very moment they were stalking me through the cactus in the growing darkness.

Fearful and confused, I did not sleep that night, but instead spent the night sitting on a hillside above my camper with my high-powered rifle across my knees. There was enough light that night so that I had a wide field of view. In the morning I cautiously made my way up to where I had last seen the car and its two occupants. I found nothing. There were no skidmarks, no wreckage, and no side roads where a vehicle could have turned off. Not only that, the banks at the side of the road at that spot were too high even for a four-wheel drive to cross.

I spent years relating that story to interested listeners in an effort to find anyone who might have a logical explanation. Now I am convinced that the incident was somehow UFO-related.

I have read of people in other places who have had similar unnerving sightings. It's quite an experience to witness something like that, especially alone in a desert twenty miles from the nearest telephone.

CHAPTER 14

Alternative Three

Two important UFO-related documents that I will briefly summarize in this chapter are the book *Alternative Three* by Leslie Watkins (published by Avon in 1978) and a lengthy paper by Bill Cooper, which will soon become a book (see bibliography).

Copies of *Alternative Three* have all but disappeared, with the exception of underground photocopied versions available in some of the more courageous New Age bookstores. The book *Alternative Three* is in great demand in progressive circles, but it seems that pressure on publishers past, present and future to cease and desist is coming from some government source. Even book-search companies, which normally carry or duplicate works such as *Alternative Three*, cannot presently locate or produce even one copy in any form.

The future may prove both of these documents to be in error. But at the moment evidence and independent testimony largely indicates that both of these works are fundamentally true, as inconceivable as what they postulate may seem to be.

*

Bill Cooper is an honorably discharged U.S. military officer who saw lengthy combat in Vietnam as captain of a river patrol boat. He was later assigned to Naval Intelligence on the CINCPACFLT staff in the Pacific. His duty was to brief admirals and other high-ranking naval officers on matters of urgency and of the highest security, including UFO activity. During this Pacific duty, he was exposed to supersecret government documents that indicated that the government considered UFOs to be of the highest priority.

At the time of his personal exposure to these documents, he began a one-man probe to discover what the depth of the government's involvement was, and what was really going on.

Prior to Cooper's intelligence duty he had been stationed on the USS Tiru. The Tiru is a submarine that was at that time based in Pearl Harbor.

While on a cruise from the Portland-Seattle area, Cooper and four seamen, including the captain of the submarine, watched an aircraft-carrier-sized UFO exiting and reentering the sea several times near the sub. This occurrence was photographed by one of the officers.

Upon returning to Pearl Harbor, Cooper and the others, except for the captain, were interrogated by a plainclothes intelligence officer. They were intimidated by the man, who said that they would be "very good" sailors if they forgot the whole affair.

Because of the urgency of the UFO question, Mr. Cooper has felt compelled by conscience to come forward with what he has learned. Bill Cooper is justifiably on constant alert for attempts that might be made on his life. Recent history shows that a significant number of UFO researchers, military and nonmilitary, have either died under extremely suspicious circumstances or have had their archives stolen, never to be seen again, archives that took years of difficult and costly research.

The major points of the Cooper papers are as follows.

At the beginning of the UFO flap in the late 1940s the United States Government, through its military establishment, came into quick and successive possession of over a dozen crashed disc-shaped craft that were either wholly intact or totally demolished. They also recovered over fifty dead alien crewmen from these crafts. One alien, however, survived the 1947 Roswell, New Mexico, crash. He was found several days later wandering in the desert. They named this space being EBE (extraterrestrial biological entity). EBE was held prisoner until his death in 1949. Before his death EBE revealed a wealth of information. It is purported to be recorded, with photographs, in a volume called *The Yellow Book*. The government at that time gave UFOs a secrecy status above that of even the hydrogen bomb!

During the Eisenhower administration a supersecret group called MJ-12 was created to deal with the alien question. MJ-12 is still very much in operation today. According to Cooper, MJ-12 assassinated President John F. Kennedy when Kennedy found out what MJ-12 was really up to in its dealings with the aliens and that MJ-12 was financing its enormously expensive activities through a massive drug cartel it controlled. MJ-12 was, and is, doing this so that monies would not have to be appropriated from government funds, thus hiding its activities from public scrutiny. I (the author) and thousands of others have viewed Cooper's enlarged, slow-motion film of the Kennedy assassination in Dallas in 1963. The film shows the driver, Secret Service agent William Greer, turning in the driver's seat and, with a shiny cylinder in his left hand, apparently shooting Kennedy in the head.

Bill Cooper has publicly accused Secret Service agent William Greer of the murder of President Kennedy. Cooper has neither been sued nor has he heard from any branch of the U.S. government in reply to this matter.

The Cooper paper states that in 1954, MJ-12 and some segments of the government secretly established a treaty with an alien race, and later found that the aliens were not living up to that agreement. It was then that MJ-12 realized it had made a horrible mistake. It was debated within the inner circles of the government whether to reveal the truth to the public or to clamp down even tighter on the secrecy of the project. The latter was decided upon, as they felt public reprisal and panic would be uncontrollable. In short, according to the paper, we have been lied to and deceived by our own government.

Some further points of Cooper's paper are:

1. The aliens have several large underground bases in the Four Corners area of Colorado, Utah, Nevada and Arizona.

2. They have been systematically abducting and performing experiments on American citizens for decades.

3. There is a joint U.S./alien base at Groom Lake, Nevada, which is in the center of a vast military reservation north of Las Vegas. At this underground base the U.S. is utilizing alien technology given to them by the aliens in exchange for the government's noninterference with their activities on Earth.

4. MJ-12 and associated agencies are now in complete control of the U.S. government.

5. There is now a herculean effort on the part of the U.S. government to develop a nuclear device carried by a missile that would be effective against underground alien bases. This nuclear device would penetrate 3,000 feet of hard desert soil such as is found in New Mexico. This device is called Excalibur and the project is under the direction of Dr. Edward Teller, the same man who is called the "father of the hydrogen bomb."

6. MJ-12 forced President Nixon to resign, counter to his ambitions, fearing that an impeachment trial would ultimately uncover their activities.

7. The U.S. has successfully developed a beam weapon called Joshua. This weapon is said to be effective against alien ships.

These are the major points of the Cooper papers. The minor points are equally interesting.

It now appears, and I don't state this lightly, that we do indeed have a beam weapon capable of shooting down alien spacecraft. It seems this weapon has already been used more than once. It may be that this, or yet another type of beam weapon, was used to shoot down an alien craft at 1:59 p.m. on May 7, 1989, over the Botswana Desert in South Africa. There were allegedly alien survivors, who with their ship are now reported to be at Wright-Patterson Air Force Base.

My question is, if this information is accurate—when are they going to start shooting back? (If they haven't already.) There are reliable reports in military circles of deadly skirmishes with UFOs.

In a more recent development, a physicist employed by the U.S. government has appeared on television and claims the government is test-flying captured (or donated) alien spacecraft at the supersecret facility at Groom Lake, Nevada. Groom Lake is 85 miles north of Las Vegas and is in the center of the enormous Nellis Air Force Range. He claims to have personally seen these alien ships and has witnessed them flying, although he has not seen the pilots. He also states that he personally viewed a disc-shaped craft that looked as though it had been hit by some sort of projectile. He saw an entrance hole in the bottom of the ship and a mushroomed-out exit hole in the top of the ship.

ALTERNATIVE THREE—THE BOOK

In 1957 a symposium, or think tank, was convened in New York to discuss the current state of the planet. This symposium was attended by many of the world's greatest scientific minds. These intellectuals reached the conclusion that the Earth would self-destruct by or shortly after the year 2000 due to overpopulation and man's relentless destruction of Earth's resources and its environment.

The U.S. government, noting these findings, conducted its own research on the matter. The findings of the symposium received further subsequent confirmation. A plan was then formulated by President Eisenhower and various individuals and branches of government. They came up with three possible alternatives to the impending disaster, which they designated Alternatives 1, 2 and 3.

ALTERNATIVE ONE was a plan to explode nuclear devices in the upper layers of the earth's atmosphere to create holes that could release trapped heat and pollution into space. This was quickly rejected as being too risky.

ALTERNATIVE TWO was a plan to construct huge underground complexes that would house selected scientists and individuals. These individuals would carry on with human civilization after surface populations (us!) were wiped out. This plan is reported to have been in high gear for many years and has been implemented under the guise of mining, construction or other similar guises.

ALTERNATIVE THREE was a plan that would make full use of the technology and direct aid of the aliens who are the same ones involved in the 1954 treaty. The idea was to begin to evacuate from the planet appropriate scientific minds, healthy young intellectuals and others who would be guaranteed passage to bases to be built on Mars. With the help of the aliens, this was found to be totally feasible. A facility was begun on Mars in the middle 1960s. A midway station called Adam was constructed on the moon.

If it seems inconceivable that we could have bases on the moon in cooperation with the Soviets and an alien race, see the book, *We Discovered Alien Bases on the Moon*, by Fred Steckling. The photos in this book are those taken from orbiting Apollo moon flights in the late 1960s and early 1970s. These NASA photos clearly show clouds and lakes on the moon and forestlike vegetation in certain areas there. These photos also show vehicles and structures that could have been built only by beings with extraordinary technological capabilities.

The author of the book *Alternative Three*, Leslie Watkins (with David Ambrose and Christopher Miles), began his initial probe when he became aware of a remarkable "brain drain" of notable young scientists around the world. These people, according to the book, were disappearing without a trace. Many were found to have packed a bag or two on what was apparently only a few hours' notice, leaving all relatives and major possessions behind.

The antagonism between the U.S. and the Soviet Union has been an incredible charade, according to the authors. There has been a successful joint U.S./alien/USSR project beginning in the 1950s. The moon shots and the space program were and are a staggeringly expensive front designed to divert possible discovery of the true activities of conspiring agencies deep within the U.S. and Soviet governments. They needed to buy themselves time. Secrecy by clandestine agencies was further ensured by guaranteeing participating individuals a ticket off Earth when things started to get rough.

To eliminate the possibility of information leaks, top-level decision-making meetings are held by U.S. and Soviet participants on a nuclear submarine under the north polar icecap. Evidently this has not succeeded, as it seems someone on the inside has leaked certain vital aspects of these ultra-secret meetings, enough so that investigators putting two and two together have come up with a very disturbing four!

All this would make great science fiction—if it *is* only fiction. However, what if it is not at all science fiction, but accurate depictions of very real and present conditions?

Ask hard questions, and startling answers begin to surface. One does not have to dig very deep these days!

CHAPTER 15

What Can *We* Do?

We have covered a lot of ground in this book, but like many UFO books, it leaves one with the question, "So what can *we* do?" Often UFO literature leaves the reader with the hopeless feeling that the situation is out of control. There is a feeling of being preyed upon like helpless cattle by an incomprehensible force—and the belief that there is little we can do about it.

There are, in fact, at least three powerful measures we can take. The primary one is not to become trapped in fear over the alien issue and thus become embroiled in all the distress and distortions that accompany fear.

The second measure is increased awareness. Learn all you can about extraterrestrial activity here on this planet. There seems to be an element of protection in knowledge and awareness of UFO and alien activities. During my research I found that most individuals who were involuntarily involved in negative UFO encounters were those who were, for the most part, totally oblivious to the reality of the existence of off-planet alien humanoids. Those researchers who are actively pursuing UFO and alien evidence seem to be "hot potatoes"—they are being left alone by the aliens, especially if the researcher has strong spiritual beliefs.

Do we in fact have inner powers that some manipulative ETs are afraid of? I think we do. In fact, I am convinced of it. I believe when these psychic, or parapsychological, energies are activated we have an invincible protection against an alien takeover of our free will. I think these powers are backed by Universal Law and the Creator Source, which all higher intelligences must obey—even those called "the opposing forces," however one interprets the term. Do you really think a Creator would allow an evil or opposing force to exist unless there were a reason? (Namely, to teach some evolving entities—ourselves and the opposing forces—certain lessons.)

We really do not have to be subjected to an "evil" force unless (a) we want to, (b) we think we are powerless, (c) we don't believe they exist, or (d) we are completely oblivious to the whole matter.

The unfortunate truth is that we are indeed being manipulated and experimented upon by several groups of alien visitors. The simple fact is, they are real, living entities to be reckoned with, and we need to focus our attention toward this activity.

Alien visitors to this planet seem to fall into three categories. These are my conclusions: 10% are against us; 40% are indifferent and wouldn't interfere no matter what we do to ourselves, and 50% seem to be doing everything (although discreetly) they can to help us. These figures are my estimates after looking into almost every source of information I could access.

Prominent among the assisting ETs seem to be several human races of divergent planetary origins—three, I would estimate. They can and do walk among us Earth humans, for physically they look exactly like us. These are the ones I am devoting a large part of my energies in trying to contact, but I think it is basically up to them. When *they* are ready, they will.

On the negative side of this human-ET coin, there seems to be a contingency of human aliens of unknown origin who have been meddling in our affairs since Cro-Magnon man suddenly appeared from nowhere 50,000 years ago. They have kept us divided and fighting among ourselves for some reason known ultimately only by them. This discord most certainly has been to their benefit, although I have no idea (nor does anyone else) why they are playing these destructive, Machiavellian games with us in the manner they are.

One might say in frustration, "Great! This is just another problem heaped onto the ones we already have!" But is it? Here in our Earth system we have human and humanoid visitors from the stars who have advanced general knowledge and far advanced technology. Some of these groups are willing to share this information with *us*—the people—now. Not with our governments. That was tried and the aliens found that Earth governments could not be trusted.

I believe absolutely that there is an imminent way to establish direct contact of mutual integrity between alien races and us, the people, and in a manner in which all parties can compassionately benefit. And I am talking about a one-to-one basis as equals, not as superiors and inferiors. With proper information we absolutely do have the intelligence to understand who and what they are.

I can tell you what *one* of the reservations is that the aliens have in openly contacting us. (For a moment put yourself in their place, observing us from a distance. Would you be reluctant to get involved when you watch what we do to ourselves, our fellow creatures and our planet?) That one reservation is that they are fully aware of our race's propensity to create new gods and cult religions. The last thing they want (the ones we want to know) is millions upon millions of us throwing ourselves at their feet beseeching them to instantly relieve us of our problems or evacuate us off the planet. It is going to take well-grounded, honest, common-sense work on our part. If proper contact can be made, and if we can put aside greed and ego, the benefits within years can be transformational to our planet and to our species.

At this point if you are still unconvinced about what I am saying, I strongly suggest that you embark upon an investigation of the UFO/alien matter on your own. It doesn't take a fortune—but it does take time. If after much study you weigh *all* the factors in this subject, I am quite confident that you will arrive at conclusions similar to mine.

The third measure lies in that of spirituality (not religion). I believe that in spirituality, which is one's fervent desire to connect to one's Divine Source, surely lies the path to our greatest power.

There are many ways of finding the "path" to the Source, and each individual develops his or her own personal method of search. Some of these methods are through meditation, prayer, song, mantras, affirmations, group discussion, reading, channeling, straightforward desire, psychic exploration—there are many.

Everything else can wait, but our search for God cannot.

In regard to malevolent aliens, from a spiritual standpoint there are cases where individuals found themselves in a negative interaction with aliens (abduction attempt). In these particular cases, these individuals who had unshakable spiritual confidence proclaimed or affirmed that they were one with the Creator. They invoked the Light and the "angels" of the Light, and demanded that under the Universal Law of the Divine Creator the alien intruders could not violate their free will. When the belief in protection by the Creator Force was strong enough within the individual being abducted, in every instance I know of the aliens broke off the attempt and departed.

In several cases other individuals who were approached tried to bluff, but they didn't really believe deep down in a Creator or Divine Source, and they were abducted. Joining with the Creator can't be a halfway measure. I know this method works. I used it myself after a series of frightening middle-of-the-night visitations. I since have visualized myself in a bubblelike barrier of both my own and the Creator Force energy. I claimed that no being who would do me harm in any way could penetrate that barrier. I have had no further problems with either astral or alien intruders.

Here are several concluding thoughts relative to the alien presence here.

There is a new phrase making the rounds among New Agers: "He (or she) is coming from fear." Perhaps comments of that type may be directed toward this book. That often happens in cases where information uncomfortable to a few is brought forward. Notwithstanding, this alien issue is one we have to look squarely in the face and with somewhat of a pragmatic and scholarly approach, with both feet planted squarely on the ground.

Often public opinion regarding UFOs amounts to outright denial, or a mild-to-barely-believing tolerance—or fear. *This is not a fear issue!* This is excitement of the highest caliber. That is, if we take the time to research the subject and come to an understanding of what is going on. I believe that there is no more demanding issue today than that of the alien presence here on our planet. This is not a time to take a wait-and-see posture.

*

Some people these days are bored, restless and stifled. Their social lives are flat, their jobs are flat, their relationships are flat. So they turn to drugs, alcohol abuse, casual sex, etc. to make their reality more palatable. Here is something that can really spice things up. There is *nothing* boring concerning UFOs and alien beings!

Avarice and complacency will perhaps prove to be the stumbling block of a large segment of humanity—lulled by the "security" of a comfortable income, material possession or whatever. The average American who watches television forty-five hours a week will no doubt still be watching television when his ship comes in—and leaves without him.

Because of the extent of what I have discovered during my investigations of the UFO and alien presence here on Earth (and I wish I could write this in flashing neon letters), *I am at times overwhelmed and utterly amazed that there has not been some sort of loud public outcry and a loud demand to know what is going on!!*

✳

"Out there" are the Overseers, the compassionate Great Ones who watch us. Many are indeed human. They may perhaps be the most powerful, most loving in this and all universes. They *do* want to help *us*—the people. But we must recognize their existence and move toward them on our own initiative. As one contactee was told, "Take one step toward us, and we will take two steps toward you."

All of us on Earth are brothers and sisters on a one-way journey to perpetual peace, harmony and prosperity. Along the way we must lovingly and patiently reach out and help each other along.

Ideas have always been catalysts for change. Can we let the idea of being informed and aware about our space visitors take root? And through this bring about a dazzling new day for ourselves and all of humankind?

God Bless

Sedona Canyonlands

Sedona Canyonlands

Have you seen these beings?

Have you seen these beings?

Bibliography

Andrews, George C. *Extraterrestrials Among Us*, Llewellyn Publications, St. Paul, MN, 1986.

Beckley, Timothy Green. *MJ-12 and the Riddle of Hangar 18.* Inner Light Publications, New Brunswick, NJ, 1989.

Berlitz, Charles and **Moore, William L.** *The Roswell Incident.* Berkley Books, New York, 1988.

Bramley, William. *The Gods of Eden.* Dahlin Family Press, San Jose, CA, 1989.

Chatelain, Maurice. *Our Cosmic Ancestors.* Golden Temple Productions, Sedona, AZ, 1988.

Cooper, William. *Behold a Pale Horse.* Light Technology Publishing, P.O. Box 1495, Sedona, AZ 86336. (Publication date September 1, 1990)

Dongo, Tom. *The Mysteries of Sedona, the New Age Frontier.* Tom Dongo, Sedona, AZ, 1988.

Fawcett, Lawrence and **Greenwood, Barry J.** *Clear Intent.* Prentice Hall, Englewood Cliffs, NJ, 1984.

Fowler, Raymond E. *The Andreasson Affair.* Bantam Books, New York, 1980.

Gritz, Lt. Col. James "Bo." *A Nation Betrayed.* Center for Action, 711 Yucca St., Boulder City, NV 89005, c. 1987.

Hopkins, Budd. *Intruders.* Ballantine Books, New York, 1987.

Kinder, Gary. *Light Years.* Pocket Books, New York, 1988.

Silva, Charles A. *Date with the Gods.* Living Waters Publishing, Pontiac, MI, 1977.

Sitchin, Zecharia. *The Wars of Gods and Men.* Avon Books, New York, 1985.

Spalding, Baird T. *Life and Teaching of the Masters of the Far East.* Devorss and Company, Marina del Rey, CA, 1927.

Steckling, Fred. *We Discovered Alien Bases on the Moon.* Fred Steckling, Vista, CA, 1981.

Steiger, Brad. *The UFO Abductors.* Berkley Books, New York, 1988.

Strieber, Whitley. *Communion.* Avon Books, New York, 1987.

Strieber, Whitley. *Transformation.* Avon Books, New York, 1989.

UFO Magazine, Box 355, Los Angeles, CA 90035.

Underwood, Lila Lee. 2675 W. Hwy 89A Suite 1163, Sedona, AZ 86336.

Watkins, Leslie. *Alternative Three.* Avon Books, New York, 1978. (out of print)

Yogananda, Paramahansa. *Autobiography of a Yogi.* Self Realization Fellowship, Los Angeles, 1946.

ORDERING BOOKS BY TOM DONGO

_____ autographed copies of *The Alien Tide* @ $7.95 $_____

_____ autographed copies of *The Mysteries of Sedona* @ $6.95 $_____

Enclose first-class postage & handling as follows:
$2.00 for first book, $1.00 ea. thereafter $_____

TOTAL ENCLOSED $_____

These rates apply to the U.S.A. only. For orders outside the U.S., please write for rates.

Name _____

Address _____

_____

Send your check or money order to:
Mysteries of Sedona
P.O. Box 2571
Sedona, AZ 86336